The Author

ETHEL WILSON was born in Port Elizabeth, South Africa, in 1888. She was taken to England at the age of two after her mother died. Seven years later her father died, and in 1898 she came to Vancouver to live with her maternal grandmother. She received her teacher's certificate from the Vancouver Normal School in 1907 and taught in many local elementary schools until her marriage in 1921.

In the 1930s Wilson published a few short stories and began a series of family reminiscences which were later transformed into *The Innocent Traveller*. Her first published novel, *Hetty Dorval*, appeared in 1947, and her fiction career ended fourteen years later with the publication of her story collection, *Mrs. Golightly and Other Stories*. Through her compassionate and often ironic narration, Wilson explores in her fiction the moral lives of her characters.

For her contribution to C———————— ————lson was awarded the C——————— ————————— and the Lorne Pierce M———————————————nada in 1964. Her husb—————————————————————er later years in seclusio—————————

Ethel Wilson ——————————

ETHEL WILSON

Swamp Angel

With an Afterword by George Bowering

M&S

In accordance with the author's wishes, the text is reprinted from the
American edition, published in 1954 by Harper & Brothers Publishers.

Published by arrangement with Macmillan of Canada

New Canadian Library edition 1990

Library and Archives Canada Cataloguing in Publication

Wilson, Ethel, 1888–1980
Swamp angel

(New Canadian library)
ISBN 0-7710-8958-9

I. Title   II. Series.

PS8545.I62S8 1990   C813'.54   C90-093896-X
PQ9199.3.W5S8 1990

We acknowledge the financial support of the Government of Canada
through the Book Publishing Industry Development Program and that of
the Government of Ontario through the Ontario Media Development
Corporation's Ontario Book Initiative. We further acknowledge the
support of the Canada Council for the Arts and the Ontario Arts Council
for our publishing program.

Printed and bound in Canada

McClelland & Stewart Ltd.
The Canadian Publishers
481 University Avenue
Toronto, Ontario
M5G 2E9
www.mcclelland.com/NCL

7 8 9 10   09 08 07 06 05

Note:
   "Swamp Angel. An 8-inch, 200-pound ... gun, mounted in a swamp by the Federals, at the siege (1863) of Charleston, S. C." – *Webster's Dictionary*.
   Subsequently, there was an issue of small revolvers, inscribed "Swamp Angel."

One

T EN TWENTY fifty brown birds flew past the window and then a few stragglers, out of sight. A fringe of Mrs. Vardoe's mind flew after them (what were they – birds returning in migration of course) and then was drawn back into the close fabric of her preoccupations. She looked out over the small green garden which would soon grow dark in evening. This garden led down a few steps to the wooden sidewalk; then there was the road, dusty in fine weather; next came the neighbors' houses across the road, not on a level with her but lower, as the hill declined, so that she was able to look over the roofs of these houses to Burrard Inlet far below, to the dark green promontory of Stanley Park, to the elegant curve of the Lions' Gate Bridge which springs from the Park to the northern shore which is the base of the mountains; and to the mountains. The mountains seemed, in this light, to rear themselves straight up from the shores of Burrard Inlet until they formed an escarpment along the whole length of the northern sky. This escarpment looked solid at times, but certain lights disclosed slope behind slope, hill beyond hill, giving an impression of the mountains which was fluid, not solid.

Mrs. Vardoe had become attached to, even absorbed into the sight from the front-room window of inlet and forest and mountains. She had come to love it, to dislike it, to hate it, and at seven-fifteen this evening she proposed to leave it and not to return. Everything was, she thought, in order.

Behind her unrevealing gray eyes of candor and peace she had arranged with herself that she would arrive at this very evening and at this place where, on Capitol Hill, she would stand waiting with everything ready. There had been time enough in which to prepare. She had endured humiliations and almost unbearable resentments and she had felt continual impatience at the slowness of time. Time, she knew, does irrevocably pass and would not fail her; rather she might in some unsuspected way fail time. Her look and habit had not betrayed her although she had lived more and more urgently through the last few weeks when an irrational fear had possessed her that she – or he – would become ill, would meet with an accident, that some car, some fall, some silly bodily ailment would, with utmost indignity and indifference, interfere; but nothing had happened to interfere. The time was now half past five. It was not likely that the unlikely – having so far held its hand – would happen within two hours, but, if it did, she was armed against revealing herself and she would build in time again, or again, like the bird who obstinately builds again its destroyed nest. So strong was the intention to depart.

She had been most vulnerable and desperate when, more than a year ago, she had taken a small box of fishing flies to the shop known by sportsmen up and down the Pacific coast.

"May I see Mr. Thorpe or Mr. Spencer?"

"There's no Mr. Thorpe. I am Mr. Spencer."

"Here are some flies, Mr. Spencer."

He picked up each fly and scrutinized it. Turning it this way and that he looked for flaws in the perfection of the body, the hackle, the wings. There were no flaws. He looked up at the pleasant young woman with less interest than he felt in the flies. There were small and large flies, dun-colored flies, and flies with a flash of iridescent green, scarlet, silver.

"Who made these flies?"

"I did."

"Who taught you?"

"My father."

"Where did he learn?"

"At Hardy's."

Mr. Spencer now regarded the young woman with some respect. She was unpretentious. Her gray eyes, rimmed with dark lashes, were wide set and tranquil and her features were agreeably irregular. She was not beautiful; she was not plain. Yes, perhaps she was beautiful. She took no pains to be beautiful. The drag of her cheap cloth coat and skirt intimated large easy curves beneath.

"Would you like to sell us your flies?"

"Yes, but I have no more feathers."

"We can arrange that. Have you a vise?"

"Yes, my father's vise."

"We will take all the flies you can make. Would you like to work here? We have a small room at the back with a good light."

"I would rather work at home."

"Where do you live?"

"Out Capitol Hill way."

"And you come from . . . ?"

"I have lived in Vancouver for some time."

"Oh. You were not born . . . ?"

"I was born in New Brunswick."

"Will you come to the desk? Sit down."

He took up a pen. "Your name?"

"Lloyd." The word Vardoe died in her mouth.

He looked at her large capable hands and saw the ring.

He smiled. "You won't mind me saying, Mrs. Lloyd, but I always back large hands or even short stubby hands for tying flies."

She looked down at her hands as if she had not noticed them before. "Yes," she said, "they are large," and she looked up and smiled for the first time, a level easy smile.

"Your telephone number?"

"There is no telephone."

"Oh, then your address?"

"I'd rather call on Mondays."

He pushed his lips out and looked at her over his glasses.

"Oh," she said, "I know. The feathers. Please trust me the first few times and then I'll pay for my own."

"No, no," he protested. "Oh no, you must do whatever suits you best."

"It suits me best," she said, coloring a very little, "to call on Monday mornings and bring the flies I've made, and see what you want done for the next week and take away the material."

"That suits me too. What do you know about rods?"

"Not as much as I know about flies. But I can splice a rod, and mend some kinds of trout rods."

"Would you want to take the rods home too?"

She hesitated. "No, if I do rods, I must do them here. But I would like to do all the work you can give me . . . if I can arrange to do it."

That was how it had begun and she had been so clever; never a bright feather blew across the room; vise, hooks, jungle cock and peacock feather were all ingeniously hidden, and Edward had never known. The curtains, drawn widely, now framed her in the window as she looked out and out over the scene which she had loved and which she hoped not to see again.

In the woodshed by the lane was her canvas bag packed to a weight that she could carry, and a haversack that she could carry on her shoulders. There was her fishing rod. That was all. How often she had lived through these moments – which had now arrived and did not stay – of standing at the window; of turning; of walking through to the kitchen; of looking at the roast in the oven; of looking, once more, to see that her navy-blue raincoat with the beret stuffed in the pocket hung by the kitchen door, easy to snatch on her way out into the dark; of picking up the bags and the rod inside the woodshed door as quickly as if it were broad daylight because she had learned their place so well; of seeing the light in the Chinaman's taxi a few yards up the lane; of quickly entering the taxi on seeing the slant face of the Chinese boy; and then the movement forward. She had carefully planned the time, early enough to arrive; too late to be seen, recognized, followed, and found.

Now she advanced, as planned, along these same minutes that had so often in imagination solaced her. When, in the night, as had soon happened after their marriage, she lay humiliated and angry, she had forced her mind forward to this moment. The secret knowledge of her advancing plan was her only restoration and solace. Often, in the day and in the night, she had strengthened herself by naming, item by item, the contents of her haversack and bag. She would, in fancy, pack a sweater, her shoes ... the little vise and some flies.... How many scores of times, as her hands lay still, she had packed these little bags. Each article, as she in fancy picked or discarded it, comforted her and became her familiar companion and support. And last night she had lain for the last time beside her husband and he did not know that it was the last time.

She had once lived through three deaths, and – it really seemed – her own. Her country had regretted to inform her that her husband, Tom Lloyd, was killed in action; their child was stricken, and died; her father, who was her care, had died; and Maggie Lloyd, with no one to care for, had tried to save herself by an act of compassion and fatal stupidity. She had married Edward Vardoe who had a spaniel's eyes. Now she was to disappear from Edward's eyes.

Mrs. Vardoe, still standing at the window, raised her left hand and saw that the time was now a quarter to six. She turned and went through to the kitchen. She took her large apron from the chair where she had thrown it, tied it so that it covered her, opened the oven door, took out the roast, put the roast and vegetables back into the oven, and began to make the gravy in the pan. These actions, which were familiar and almost mechanical, took on, tonight, the significance of movement forward, of time felt in the act of passing, of a moment being reached (time always passes, but it is in the nature of things that we seldom observe it flowing, flying, past). Each action was important in itself and, it seemed, had never been real before.

The front door opened and was shut with a bang and then there was silence. As she stirred the gravy she knew what Edward was doing. He was putting his topcoat on its hanger, turning his hat in his hand, regarding it, reshaping it, and hanging them both up – the good topcoat and respectable hat of Eddie Vardoe, E. Thompson Vardoe. It's a good thing I'm going *now*, she thought as she stirred the gravy. I'm always unfair, now, to Edward. I hate everything he does. He has only to hang up his hat and I despise him. Being near him is awful. I'm unfair to him in my heart always whatever he is doing, but tonight I shall be gone.

As he walked to the kitchen door she looked up from her stirring. He stood beside her, trim, prim, and jaunty in the little kitchen. He was in rare good humor, and excited.

"Well," he said, "I pretty near bought it. Guess I'll settle tomorrow. Four hundred cash and easy terms."

She straightened herself and looked mildly at him. Was it possible that what she was about to do was not written plain on her brow.

"If you gointa show people real estate," he said, "you gotta have the right car. Something conservative but snappy. Snappy but reefined. See."

"Yes, oh yes," she agreed. She had forgotten about the car.

He took off his coat, revealing a tie on which athletes argued in yellow and red. That tie, and other ties, were new signs of Edward's advancement and self-confidence. What a tie, thought Mrs. Vardoe, stirring mechanically. When Edward took off his coat a strong sweet sour smell was released. He took a paper from an inner pocket, went to the hall and hung up his coat. He came back to the kitchen and held out the paper to her.

"Take a look at that, woodja," he said with a smile of triumph. "'E. Thompson Vardoe' – sounds all right, doesn't it!"

"Just a minute till I put the roast on the table," she said, picking up the hot platter.

He turned and followed her into the room. "Well," he said aggrieved, "I'd think you'd be innerested in your husband starting in business for himself!"

She went with her usual light deliberation into the kitchen again, brought in the vegetables, gravy, and plates, took off her apron and sat down at the table.

"Let me see it," she said.

Mr. Vardoe, sitting down in his shirt sleeves before the roast, passed her a piece of paper with a printed heading. She read aloud "Weller and Vardoe – Real Estate – Specialists in Homes – West End, Point Gray and Southern Slope – Octavius Weller, E. Thompson Vardoe."

"Oh it does look nice! I hope that . . . "

"*Say!*" said Mr. Vardoe in an affronted tone, holding the carving knife and fork above the roast of beef. "Whatever got into you, buying this size roast for two people! Must be all of six pounds! Is it six pounds?"

"No," said Mrs. Vardoe with her wide gentle look upon the roast, "but it's all of five pounds."

"And solid meat!" said Mr. Vardoe, striking the roast with the carving knife. His voice rose shrill with anger. "You buying six-pound roasts when I gotta get a new car and get started in a new business! Bet it wasn't far off a dollar a pound!"

"No, it wasn't," admitted Mrs. Vardoe. She gave a quick look down at her watch. The time was twenty minutes past six. It seemed to her that time stood still, or had died.

"It'll be nice cold," she said, without self-defense.

"Nice *cold!*" he echoed. "Who wants to eat cold meat that cost the earth for a week!"

If you only knew it, *you* will, thought Mrs. Vardoe.

Edward Vardoe gave her one more glare. In annoyed silence he began to carve the roast.

As Mrs. Vardoe put vegetables onto the two plates she dared to give another downward glance. Twenty-five minutes past six. The roast was delicious. When Edward Vardoe had shown enough displeasure and had satisfied himself that his wife had felt his displeasure he began eating and talking of his partner Octavius Weller, a man experienced – he said – in the real estate business.

"Octavius's smart all right," he said with satisfaction and his mouth full. "Anyone have to get up pooty early to fool Octavius. I guess we'll be a good team, me and O.W." He at last pushed his plate aside. He continued to talk.

Mrs. Vardoe got up and took away the meat course and brought in a pudding. Her husband looked at her strangely. He took his time to speak.

"Well, say," he said at last, "you got your good tweed suit on!"

"Yes, I have," she said, looking down at it. The time was twenty minutes to seven. She had to control a trembling in her whole body.

"Cooking a dinner in your good suit!"

"I had my apron."

"Well, what you got it *on* for! You never sit down in your good suit like that before! Wearing that suit around the house!"

She could conceal – how well she could conceal! – but she could not deceive and she did not need to deceive.

"I wanted to see Hilda and her mother. I went there and they weren't in. So I walked around for a bit and went back there and they weren't in, so I came home."

"*And* never took that suit off, and went and cooked dinner in that suit!" (That suit, that suit, that suit.)

Yes, but, her mind said, if I didn't wear my suit I hadn't room to pack it. That was all arranged. Long ago that was arranged, arranged by night, arranged by day. I won't tell him any lies. I can stay quiet a little longer whatever says. She ate her pudding mechanically, hardly knowing what she did or what he said. It all depends on me, now, she thought. If I can manage the next quarter of an hour? Oh God help me. Just this quarter of an hour. Time could kill a person, standing still like this. A person could die.

"Any more pudding?" she said.

He shook his head. Ill temper made his face peevish.

"Gimme the paper," he said sourly.

"It's here." She passed it to him and her heart beat like a clock.

He turned himself from the table and seemed to settle to the paper. A weight lifted a little from her. She took out the plates, cleared the table, and went into the kitchen, closing the door behind her. She ran the water into the dishpan. Water makes more noise than anything but crumpling paper, doesn't it, she thought. I must have things quiet, so that I can listen both ways. She piled the dishes, one on one, very quietly. It was seven o'clock. She began to wash the dishes, silently enough. The moments became intolerable. A person could die, waiting for a minute to come. She could not bear it. She dried her hands on her apron and threw off the apron. It dropped to the floor. She snatched the raincoat off the peg by the door. She slipped her arms into the raincoat and went out into the dark. If it's not here, she thought in her fluttering mind, what shall I do. If he comes into the kitchen and I have to go back in, what'll I do. The taxi might be two or three minutes early. It *might*. She walked quickly down the little back garden path to the lane where the woodshed stood. The air, cool and fresh and dark after the warm lighted kitchen, blew upon her face. She saw up the dark lane a car standing, its engine running. The absurd fear nearly choked her that this might not, after all, be her car. Some other car might be standing there. Ducking into the woodshed, she picked up the two bags and the thin fishing rod in the case, slung the haversack over her shoulder, and began to run. She reached the taxi and looked eagerly in. She saw the Chinese face. Before the driver could reach the door handle, she wrenched the door open, sprang in and closed it.

"Drive," she said, and leaned back in the car with a relief that made her for a moment dizzy.

Two

YOU CAN drive from Vancouver to New Westminster along a highway bright with motor hotels, large motorcar parks, small shops, factories of various sizes. At night everything is bright with lights and neon dazzle. In the daytime you will see that some of these motor hotels are set in old orchards, and among the rows of neat homogeneous dwellings stand old cherry trees, sprawling and frothing with white blossoms in the spring. Later, when the blossoms fall, the gnarled trees in their ingenuous beauty remind the urbanites and suburbanites, speeding past, of another kind of place. The delicate impression is crowded out and vanishes, obliterated by every modern convenience.

There is a second way that lies between Vancouver and New Westminster. It is called the river road. The river is the Fraser River, never far distant from the road. On the high north side of the road there is still some forest or large bush, and there is the agreeable illusion that the few pleasant and rustic small houses that stand alone amongst the trees above the road are really permanent in their aloneness, so that the road will keep its intrinsic quality of appearing to be far removed from a city. But over the ridge that descends to the road the city of Vancouver is crawling on. Bulldozers are leveling the small trees and laying bare a pale and stony soil. The landscape is being despoiled, as it must, on behalf of groups of small houses, a golf course, schools, a cemetery, all the amenities of living, learning, playing, and dying. The north side of the river road has no intrinsic quality of permanence after all, we see, and will soon be just another road, but the river flows below the south side and commands the scene.

The Chinese taxi in which Mrs. Lloyd escaped from her discarded but still lawful husband E. Thompson Vardoe followed neither of these roads. The Chinese boy drove along secondary roads which were very dark, being lighted at intervals only by lamps shining in the windows of small frame houses built in clearings by the roadside. He turned south toward a third highway leading to New Westminster which was the nearest main road to the home of his passenger and which had no special characteristics. It was simply a road built through an undulating country, sparsely settled. This countryside will, however, soon be thickly populated, as it is the only direction in which Vancouver can expand. Vancouver lies on a tongue of land, a promontory, and cannot expand to the north, for there is Burrard Inlet and the mountains; it cannot expand to the west, because there is the Gulf of Georgia; it cannot expand to the south, for there is the Fraser River, and the delta islands with airport and farms. So it will have to expand to the east, meeting eventually with the town of New Westminster. It was toward this highway that the Chinese taxi was headed when the passenger called suddenly "Stop."

The young Chinese taxi driver made an abrupt movement and stopped the car. He turned a startled earnest face.

"Are we still inside the city limits?" asked his passenger.

He considered. "No," he said.

"Turn back till we're just inside the city limits, mail this letter, turn round and keep on going to New Westminster – but keep away from where you picked me up."

He looked at her curiously and took the letter.

"Okay," he said.

The passenger seemed to sit stiff and erect until the boy

had drawn up by a dim roadside, mailed the letter, slipped back into the car, turned around and proceeded on his way.

Then she relaxed, sighing.

Three

THE FORWARD movement of the taxi through the dark was separating Mrs. Lloyd as did every moment of passing time from the house that had been called her home. Time slid behind her – she could feel it and count it – and the road slid behind her, and the fixed point of the house which still contained Edward Vardoe became more irrevocably far away. Each approaching and passing car whose lights grew, blazed, passed and were no more, each house whose faintly lighted bulk neared and vanished, each distantly spaced and passed country light, the continuous noise of the engine of the taxi – all these innocent accompaniments of travel through the night were full of meaning and assumed their places as elements on her side in her flight from Edward Vardoe. Just as, if the Chinese driver had turned his car again and for some reason had performed the easy physical feat of driving back to the house where he had picked her up, each of these elements would have contributed to her calamity.

Before this moment she had had on her side only her own private determination and her outraged endurance of the nights' hateful assaults and the days' wakings in a passing of time where daily and nightly repetition marked no passing of time. Only the calendar, watched often enough, could mark it, and the small pile of bills, the earned secret money which grew slowly and grew until changed for larger bills, and then grew again. But now each new minute in the taxicab was as jubilant as the cry of a trumpet. Everything was on her side. She exulted in each small sight and sound, in new time, in new space, because now she had got free.

Mrs. Lloyd, sitting gloriously alone in the back seat of the car, regarded the dark shape of the young driver in front of her. Even the choice of the Chinese taxi had contributed to her security. If, that night, less than half an hour ago and a lifetime away, she had found what she called a "white" taxi waiting in the lane, minutes might have been lost in argument, for some other car might by coincidence have been waiting there. But when she had seen in the fragmented light the slant face of the Chinese boy, she did not need to ask; she knew that her plan was falling into its place, and she and the taxi moved quickly away from Edward Vardoe, according to plan.

Her face took on its generous easy curves in the dark in contemplation of the day a few weeks ago when she had first seen the young Chinaman who now sat in front of her. The day had been wet. Rain had fallen steadily and the east end of Vancouver bore its own look of drenched sameness. Mrs. Lloyd, wearing the blue belted raincoat which now she wore in the moving taxi, with the hood pulled over her head, had walked briskly with her hands in her pockets, facing west on Pender Street, facing – that is – toward that section of Pender Street which shows you by the kind of buildings which you pass and by the monosyllabic names on these buildings that, unmistakably, you are approaching Chinatown. Chinatown intensifies and becomes its true self – and none other – just after you cross Main Street as you journey west. A short few blocks, and Chinatown ceases abruptly as if it had never been, the vestiges of Shanghai Alley are left behind, the city takes over again, regardless.

Mrs. Lloyd remembered looking to right and left of her as she walked. She remembered savoring the names above the small shops, the discreet shabby places of business, and the little live-poultry markets. Her pleasures were few, and were not communicable, and she had long formed the habit of seeking and finding, where she could, private enjoyment of the sort that costs nothing but an extension of the imagination. So when she saw the names Gum Yuen, Foo Moy, Jim Sing, Hop Wong, Shu Leong, which now came vaguely into her mind again as in a picture taken up and put down, those syllables ravished her as with scents and sounds of unknown lives and far places. Hemmed in between two squat and aged gray wooden houses was a small shabby building not unlike a church, whose open door showed, so early, a small bulb of light in a dark hall within. A shriveled Chinaman, leaning on a stick, walked along a duck-board approach, took his immortal soul inside, and vanished. Mrs. Lloyd paused to read a tablet on the church wall. Black words turning gray on a weatherworn board announced Christ's Chinese Church in Canada. Mrs. Lloyd's imagination followed the old Chinaman into the low building, back to his crowded home perhaps two streets away, and again into the church. What called him there? What were his thoughts? Who were his friends? How did he live? What were his hopes? When the church members gathered in that dingy building, what Christ did they see before them? Was Christ a Chinaman, a Jew, a Christian? He was still Christ. All this and much more she passionately longed to know, but her mind could not follow these minds in their dark directions. She paused, too, at a live-poultry market. Quite secret – from her – were the faces of those who bought and those who sold. She considered these enigma faces but, although she thought that she could read easily the faces of her own race (but she could not), these others were sealed from her.

She crossed Main Street on that day and walked through the rain until she came to the shop where they sold the peacock feather fans. At this place she saw only Chinese on the street. Some were old and spare, with the bony temples and eye sockets, the almost somnambulist appearance of certain of the older Chinese; there were some whose brisk Westernness overlay them; nearly all of them had the immemorial look which distinguishes their race. Mrs. Lloyd, sitting, now, in the dark of the taxi with her eyes on the Chinese boy's head, entered, then, into Lee Sing's shop; she smelled the smell, felt the lure in the air, bought the smallest of the peacock feather fans, fingered and resisted the bowls of yellow, of green, of blue rice-china; then fingered and bought one small six-sided yellow bowl. It seemed to her that she held in her hand all beauty in a cheap yellow Chinese bowl. (I shall take it with me, she had thought, and now it lay in the bag at her feet.) She went out of the store, and saw there the young Chinaman who was now driving her.

He stood at the curb of the pavement beside a taxi. It looked as though he and the taxi belonged to one another, as they did. His nonchalant attitude had a certain grace. He was waiting for someone. He stepped quickly and lightly across the pavement to where an elderly Chinese woman, dressed in black, appeared in a doorway. There was, Mrs. Lloyd had thought, a sort of swagger, a down-town arrogance in his movements. He bent over the woman who appeared to be lame. Composed, dignified, she handed him her parcels; he took her arm, escorted her across the pavement, helped her into the car, closed the door and returned with his quick yet lounging tread, his almost animal tread, to a small office out of whose door-way the elderly woman had come. Mrs. Lloyd stood, uncertain, interested. Only the need of the peacock fea-thers had brought her to Chinatown and so, for a few minutes to spare, she stood looking at the windows full of Chinese artifacts, at the people reflected in the windows, and at the people in the street. The young man talked and listened to an older Chinaman who stood in the doorway. They talked in Chinese and without gesture. The young man took his orders with a sort of brashness, nodded, and said "Okay."

"Okay, Joey," said the older man. The young man strode lightly across the pavement, slipped behind the steering wheel of the car and drove off. The older man stood in the doorway, looking up and down the street. He was fat, bland, amused, and his face was the pleasing color of smooth old ivory.

Mrs. Lloyd looked at the window beside the open door and saw the words Universal Taxi, and a telephone number. The Chinaman's bland intelligent eyes saw her inclusively and moved on. A smile broke over Mrs. Lloyd's face. The completion of her plan lay before her. She went toward the man.

"May I come in?" she asked.

"Sure, lady." And he moved aside to let her pass.

So, as she sat in the car which had now reached the outskirts of New Westminster, the peacock feather fan, the small yellow bowl, the youth whose qualities she had seen in his four times crossing the pavement, her unquestioned agreement with his father – all joined to make her departure un-strange, familiar, and were part of her happiness.

The taxi drew up at the bus station. She got out, and the driver handed her the knapsack which she slung on her shoulder, gave her the handbag and the slender case with the fishing rod.

"Going fishing?" he asked. The usual question.

"Yes, I am," she said pleasantly.

She paid him, said "Good-by Joey, and thank you," went into the open station and sat down. There was some time to wait. Mrs. Lloyd felt suddenly tired. She slipped her pack aside, leaned back and closed her eyes.

She heard a voice. "You all right, lady?"

She opened her eyes and saw the young Chinaman standing there. He looked down as he rolled a cigarette.

"You're not sick, are you?"

"No," she said, "I'm all right. I think I'm a little tired but I'm not ill."

He looked at the station clock.

"You got fifteen minutes. Don't you think," tentatively, " . . . a cuppa coffee . . . ?"

She rose to her feet and said gratefully "Oh yes let's!" and they went together to the coffee counter.

"I didn't mean ... " the young man said awkwardly, "that I ... that you gotta ... "

"Oh Joey," said Mrs. Lloyd, "you don't know how glad I am! This is a queer journey I'm on," he nodded, "and it's nice to start it like this ... with a new friend, I mean."

The hot coffee was put before them and they sipped, not speaking.

Then – "Joey," said Mrs. Lloyd suddenly, "do you know what?"

"What," said the boy.

"I don't know where I'm going, but I know the kind of place I want to find and I know what I want to do. I want to have a certain kind of business. I know what I want. I've worked it all out and I know I can do it. But there's one thing missing. Maybe I'll find it up-country and maybe I won't. I'll need a partner with a good head who's got a car and who's a good driver. To go halvers or nearly halvers." She looked at the boy and her calm eyes held new interest in him. His face, she thought, had not a secret look. She thought that she understood him and that East and West blended in him in a way that seemed open to her. Perhaps he was now more Canadian than Chinese. By certain processes he was both.

The boy's upper lip lifted in a smile that gave his face a fastidious expression (like a young priest, like a young lord, like a young tiger, she thought), and looked away across the coffee bar to the placarded advertisements that covered the wall – advertisements so familiar, so blatant, that the eye no longer saw them and the mind no longer read them. He stared not at but through the placards without speaking. Then he looked quickly at his wrist watch.

"Did you mean me and you ... partners ... in a business?" he asked, looking at her.

She gave a quick nod. "You don't have to say now. It

just fits in with something . . . it *does* sound crazy, doesn't it, Joey," she smiled, "but it's not."

"I guess your bus'll be coming and I gotta get going," he said evasively, "and Dad's got another call for me. I'd . . . well, I might be innerested, lady . . . it'd depend. But, well, say, I don't know your name!"

"You'd know it if I wrote to you, maybe two . . . three . . . months from now . . . maybe in a year. You'd know me. Oh . . . thank you . . . "

"Well, so long, lady," he said, standing with awkward grace.

"Good-by," she said. She forgot that she was tired. She watched him vanishing, slipping neatly through the crowd. She walked toward the bus which now stood waiting.

"Is this the bus for up the Valley, for Chilliwack?" she asked.

The conductor moved an assenting hand. She got into the bus, carrying quite easily the bag, her knapsack and the fishing rod.

"Going fishing?" asked the conductor.

"Yes, I am," she said pleasantly.

Four

A SHORT TIME before Mrs. Lloyd stepped up into the bus, Edward Vardoe, having reached a boiling point of fury, found himself unable to enjoy boiling in a sitting posture any longer and leaped to his feet. In addition to the annoying incidents of the tweed suit and the roast of beef there had been something queer, an untouchableness, about his wife's manner at dinnertime. In fact, there was no "manner." She had seemed not to be, or, perhaps, to be somewhere else.

Edward Vardoe, high with grievance, marched to the door, flung it open, and looked into the kitchen. She was not there. My God, she's left the dishes, she must be dead. A few plates were washed and lay there, drained. But the meat pan was there, and the vegetable saucepans, untouched. Edward Vardoe went into the kitchen and stood, looking about him. All was still. The back door through which his wife had fled stood open. Beyond lay the dark garden and the invisible woodshed. He listened. His feelings were confused. Surprise at the simple and unusual absence of his wife allayed his anger a little. He called through the open door "Maggie!" There was no sound but a small wind flapping in the dark garden. He called more loudly "Maggie!" There was no answer. He was aware of people passing, gone, in front of the house, but, at the back, nothing except the dark. He became aware of a listening in the empty kitchen.

He turned abruptly and saw on the floor beside the sink her apron lying as if thrown down in haste. He looked at the peg where her raincoat sometimes hung. It was not there.

"Maggie!"

He went through the dining room to the row of pegs in the little hall. Her raincoat was not in its regular place, neither was her beret.

Louder. Louder. "Maggie! Maggie!"

He walked upstairs, listening as he went up step by step. The figure in the shirt sleeves rounded the turn at the top of the stairs. He turned on a light and went into the bedroom. All was the same, but different. The bedroom was listening, too.

He turned and went into the only other room and into the bathroom. No one was there. The whole small house was listening. He went back into the bedroom and opened the door of the clothes cupboard. He cleared his confused and angry mind and tried to remember which of her clothes hung customarily there. The tweed suit was, of course, gone. Her one hat was still on its shelf but something was missing. Shoes seemed to have gone. He turned and sprang to the chest of drawers. Some things (what things?) were not there. In a storm of rage he threw the remaining garments to the floor. He emptied the next drawer and the next. He rushed to the drawer where she kept her brush and comb and face powder. Empty. He dashed it to the floor. He hurried to the bathroom. His awakened suspicions could not tell. Poor human doll, running from room to room in the empty house. Oh rage, hurt pride, fury! Maggie had gone secretly out into the night. She had taken her brush and comb; and he who lived habitually on the edge of other suspicions was aware that she had left him.

Edward Vardoe did not know that he was trembling. He went downstairs. His hands and eyes seemed to prevent his finding a telephone number in the book but at last he dialed the telephone.

"You are calling the wrong number," said a flat voice. His hands, his eyes, the dial, all objects conspired against him. He dialed again, bringing the small disc down flang, flang, flang, flang.

"Hello," said Hilda Severance.

"Is she there?" he asked, and his voice shook.

'Is who there?'

"You know who!" he shouted.

"You have the wrong number," said the cool voice of Hilda Severance. He slammed down the telephone.

Lights were now burning throughout the house. He started for the front door, turned back and put on his coat. He banged the door and walked hurriedly down the wooden sidewalk.

An expanse of air in the night, endless, soft, fluent, still, blowing, moving, clearing, closing, sliding through dark leaves and branches and past houses and lampposts and black silent areas and bright areas of sound, movement and smell, separating lover from lover, victim from approaching thief, thief from hunter, mother from child, quite hid Maggie afar from Edward Vardoe who walked with prim quick steps along the shabby sidewalk in the dark on Capital Hill. As he walked, an assurance of something monstrous and impossible rose within him. Maggie had left him. His humiliation, still awaiting sure knowledge of the fact, would overwhelm him. He did not love Maggie, not as love counts for love. But she was his wife, and by God she had left him. Hardly a small space in his mind remained lighted by sense to tell him that somewhere there was a valid reason for the departure of Maggie and that it was intrinsic in him that she should go. Then that space closed up and no reason lighted his mind. He muttered "Maybe she went to ... the ... drugstore." He did not know that he talked aloud but he knew that his muttering was futile. Face powder, brush and comb, that good suit, the open door, the dropped apron, her strangeness – and by gum that big roast! – rose up and retired again after telling him coldly that Maggie had left him.

Edward Vardoe, swimming in a murky sea of emotions of hate and self-pity ("I've been done, done, had for a sucker!"), ascended the steps of a small house which showed only one light, and rang the bell.

The porch light then shone and there were lights in a room and the hall. The door was opened, and Hilda Severance stood there, dark and slim.

The sight of his wife's friend stirred the fury again in Edward Vardoe.

"Is she here?" he asked abruptly.

"Oh, it was you that telephoned!" remarked Hilda Severance.

"Sure it was me! She's here! She came here!"

Hilda Severance shook her head. "I really don't know what you're talking about but I suppose it's Maggie. You'd better come in."

Edward Vardoe walked in and they went into the little parlor. His quick glances searched the room.

"She's not here. You can look anywhere you like," said Hilda Severance, "and I don't know what you're talking about. Has Maggie gone away?"

"Gone!" he said, throwing up his hands. "She's gone."

Hilda Severance said nothing, but stood, looking at him and thinking.

"You're her friend," he said, "she talks to you! She never talks to me! She must have told you she was going! Is it a man? or . . . "

But Maggie had not the fatal gift of intimacy. Hilda Severance had long ago divined that Maggie was a quiet woman who, though not secretive, did not require to talk, to divulge, to compare, to elicit; and she had not resented this. Maggie, brought up from childhood by a man, with men, had never learned the peculiarly but not wholly feminine joys of communication, the déshabille of conversation, of the midnight confidence, the revelation. And now, serenely and alone, she had acted with her own resources, and whatever she had chosen to do, Hilda Severance was glad that Maggie had not delivered herself into the hands of a friend, even into *her* hands. Thus she knew nothing. Edward Vardoe broke into a torrent of accusation and abuse.

Mrs. Severance, sitting up in bed in her room, listened, put out her cigarette stub, got out of bed with agility considering her size, thrust her small feet into bedroom slippers, shed her shawl, put on her dressing gown, knotted the cord, reached for her package of cigarettes, and walked with ponderous softness into the parlor. She stood in the doorway and looked at Edward Vardoe without expression. She crossed the room, lowered herself into a chair, took out a cigarette, tapped it firmly, lighted it, drew heavily, and blew twin spirals through her nostrils. Through the spirals she looked at Edward Vardoe. She did not speak.

Edward Vardoe checked himself for a moment. Then, seeing that this massive woman in the armchair seemed to be only a spectator, he continued.

"She said she came here today and you were both out."

"I took some typing out to the University this afternoon, and when Mother's lying in bed she doesn't get up for anybody."

Edward Vardoe threw his arms wide.

"If there was anything wrong, why didn't she say so? If she ... if there's a man ... where would there be a man ... I been a good husband ... her wearing that good suit tonight ... I knew ... she's quiet and artful as the devil ... planned all this ... if there's a man by God I'll find her ... I'll fix her ... I'll ... "

Mrs. Severance narrowed her eyes and looked at him. She leaned across the table beside her and picked up a small nickel-plated revolver, pearl-handled. On the metal was inscribed in flowing script the words Swamp Angel. Mrs. Severance twirled the Swamp Angel as if absent-mindedly, then like a juggler she tossed it spinning in the air, caught it with her little hand, tossed it again, higher, again, higher, spinning, spinning. It was a dainty easy practiced piece of work, the big woman with the Swamp

Angel. Edward Vardoe stopped speaking and watched her, taken out of himself.

He turned to Hilda Severance. "Why does she do that?"

"She likes doing it," said Hilda equably. "That was hers, and her father's." She smiled. "That's the family pet. It's the Swamp Angel. Her father used it in the business and so did she."

"Business?"

Mrs. Severance looked coldly at her daughter.

"Can she shoot?"

Hilda Severance laughed. "You'd best go home, Mr. Vardoe," she said, "and pull yourself together. Perhaps Maggie's not gone. If she *has* gone, there's not much you can do, is there? Maggie won't change her mind. If she's gone, she won't come back. You'd better settle to that. I don't think there's a man. In fact I'm sure."

Mrs. Severance got up slowly, as one bored by proceedings, and walked ponderously back to her room, taking her cigarettes and the Swamp Angel with her. Hilda Severance continued. "Go home," she said rather kindly, "and get a night's sleep and face it all in the morning."

Edward Vardoe rose as if drunk or dreaming. He went out without a word, down the steps and along the dark road. As his thoughts outpaced him he saw the confusion of the bedroom, the pans at the kitchen sink, and – by gum – all the lights on, and him so careful. Then in the shade of tomorrow waited the new car and Mr. Weller and humiliation that only venom could assuage. His life was broken off, splintered like a stick, and she'd done it.

Mrs. Severance kicked off her little slippers and heaved herself up into the bed. She settled herself against the pillows with satisfaction and was just striking a match when her daughter came and stood in the doorway.

"You're a wicked old woman and should be ashamed of yourself," said her daughter.

"I know," said Mrs. Severance comfortably.

She pulled the shawl well round her and blew two spirals.

"You go and make a good pot of coffee," she said, "and we'll have it here. That was a sweet bit of melodrama wasn't it . . . what d'you suppose happened to Maggie? . . ."

Five

MAGGIE LLOYD who was Maggie Vardoe left the bus at Chilliwack and asked her way to the modest auto camp where she proposed to spend the night. Seventy miles away Mrs. Severance demonstrated to Edward Vardoe her art with the Swamp Angel, and three people confronted each other with strong feelings all on account of Maggie. But Maggie, as free of care or remembrance as if she had just been born (as perhaps she had, after much anguish), followed the proprietor to a small cabin under the dark pine trees. He unlocked the door, pushed it open, turned on a meager light, and looked at his customer.

"There's plenty wood and paper beside the stove if you want a fire ... there's matches ... here's the key ... the privies is back behind the cabins ... there's a light ... going fishing?"

"Yes, I am," said Maggie as she put down her gear.

"Well, good night then, I hope you sleep good."

"Good night," she said, and closed the door behind him and locked it.

As she lay in the dark in the hard double bed and smelled the sweet rough-dried sheets, she saw through the cabin windows the tops of tall firs moving slowly in a small arc, and back, against the starred sky. Slowly they moved, obliterating stars, and then revealing them. The place was very still. The only sound was the soft yet potential roar of wind in the fir trees. The cabin was a safe small world enclosing her. She put out a hand, groped on the stand beside her bed, took up the small yellow bowl, ran her thumb round its smooth glaze like a drowsy child feeling its toy. How lovely the sound of the wind in the fir trees. She fell asleep.

Six

H OPE IS a village on the forested banks of the Fraser River at a point where that river deploys dramatically from the mountains. The history of Hope goes back into the last century when it was a point of arrival, meeting, and departure for miners who were working the Fraser River bars or pressing on to the mines of the Cariboo Country, for Hudson's Bay men, and for many travelers. "Many" has a relative meaning. British Columbia's small population, scattered sparsely from the northern Rockies to west and south, and up from the coast, was centered chiefly at the southern tip of Vancouver Island, where Fort Camosun became Victoria; but there was a surge from the United States and from Vancouver Island. Because the rumor and the fact of gold drew white men and Chinamen to the Fraser River bars and further and still further north and east, and because the powerful and difficult Fraser River formed a route – not a highway – and because the Cariboo Trail (first a toehold, then an earthen trail shored up against the mountains high above the river, and now with full crescendo a fine winding well-graded motor road) followed and skipped the river's lines and curves, the village of Hope and other companion villages and forts – Yale and Langley – held importance for the small seat of government in Victoria, for the Hudson's Bay traders, for thousands of American miners, and for other people in the young colony. This bit of history is implicit in the road; it accompanies the water and the air of the river.

Hope is still a village set among noble trees on the bank of a great and wicked river, backed by ascending mountains, and until lately it retained its look of dreaming age. But the look of dreaming age has gone, and Hope lies between two forks of highroads, each going into the mountains, and is subsidiary to them. The main highroad from Vancouver, passing through Chilliwack where Maggie had spent the night, splits at the village of Hope. The northern fork follows the old Cariboo Trail along the steep banks of the Fraser River which winds in broad sweeps and narrow hairpin curves on the sides and rumps of hills and mountains growing ever nearer, ever higher, until at Hell's Gate Canyon the close rocks of the river banks confine the raging waters – and further west until the first sagebrush is seen. On goes the road to Kamloops and beyond.

For a long time past the word at the back of Maggie's mind, and at the end of her plan and her journey, had been Kamloops.

The second road, which branches at Hope, turns to the right, that is, south of the Cariboo Road and nearer to the American border. It follows the Hope-Princeton Trail (historic trail of miners and cattlemen) which is now the Hope-Princeton Highway, climbing into the mountains. Here are many streams, and the Coquihalla River, the young Skagit River, and at last the Similkameen River. The Hope-Princeton Highway, like the Cariboo Highway, moves into British Columbia's heart. It leads to a mining country, and orchard countries, past lakes, rivers and mountains into the Boundary Country fabulous with mines, with old ghost towns, with thriving communities divided by mountains and forests and waterfalling rivers, and to and beyond the mighty and mysterious concentration at Trail. This was the road that Maggie chose, at least as far as the river with the dancing name Similkameen.

Then she would turn her back on what lay beyond, return to Hope and follow, somehow, the road to Kamloops.

She was so far now from what she had left behind her on Capitol Hill that she had no fear of being overtaken. Make no mistake, when you have reached Hope and the roads that divide there you have quite left Vancouver and the Pacific Ocean. They are disproportionately remote. You are entering a continent, and you meet the continent there, at Hope.

If at any time now, Maggie thought, she should by some ridiculous calculation or miscalculation be overtaken and confronted by Edward Vardoe, she would not mind. She was Tom Lloyd's own widow again. She would not hide nor be afraid. She would not protest, upbraid, defend. She grieved a little, and helplessly, because (she thought) another woman would have done this thing better. Another woman would have faced Eddie Vardoe and told him that she could not live with him any longer. She would have left him more fairly, Maggie thought. Maggie had to go almost under his very eyes, or she would have involved her friends. She, Maggie, could not have borne the small scenes and the big scenes and the pursuit and the shoutings if she had quite faced him. She had borne the humiliations that she had borne, but she could not endure the others. He would never have let me be, she said to herself with revulsion; he would have given Hilda and her mother no peace; I know him so well. He is he, and I am I. And this was the only way for me. On a shining morning she waited for the Hope-Princeton bus at Chilliwack. She settled down beside a window.

When she first saw the Similkameen River, the dancing river with the dancing name, it was a broad mountain stream of a light blue that was silver in the bright morning, and of a silver that was blue. There was a turn in the road, and crowded somber jack pines hid the Similkameen River. There was another turn, and the river flowed laughing beside the road again. Across the rapid moving river was the forest of lodgepole pine. Shafts of sunlight smote the first trees and they stood out against the somberness and denseness of the forests behind them. Maggie looked at, but she could not look into the pine forest, for it was sealed in its density and blackness. The Similkameen River, of fairly uniform breadth, ran blue and silver and alive, level and life giving past the forests.

A sign on the roadside said "Beware of deer crossing the road." Maggie went forward to the driver. She waited until a stretch of the highway lay clear ahead and then she spoke.

"Will you set me down, please, somewhere near the river?"

The driver did not answer at once. His eyes were on the road. Then he said, "We don't usually set folks down here, lady. There's nowhere near. The next camp is a matter of some miles on."

"I shall be all right. Just set me down near the river."

The driver slowed up, and Maggie, with her gear, left the bus. The bus picked up speed and was soon out of sight. Maggie walked down to the margin of the river as in an enchantment. The pine-needle earth felt soft. She set down her gear, gazed up and down the stream, sat down, and then lay down, looking up at the sky.

Some rivers are sweet and equable. Such was the lightly dancing Similkameen River at that place, and such was Maggie lying beside it. She gave herself up to the high morning. Was she not lucky. Chipmunks watched her.

The bend of the river beside which she lay was so far from the road that the sound of the immediate rippling water filled her ears, and so she heard no sound of passing cars, and lay high up in these mountains, near the sky – it seemed – on the fringe of some open pinewoods. Something had happened, she thought as she lay there, to her sense of smell. It had become vitiated. But now her breath drank and drank again the scent of firs and pines and juniper. Time dissolved, and space dissolved, and she smelled again the pinewoods of New Brunswick, one with these woods, a continent away, and she was all but a child again. No, she was nothing. No thought, no memories occupied her. The clouds that drifted across the blue drifted through her mind as she lay idle. She sat up at last, and, looking round, saw a doe standing by a tree trunk, regarding her. The lovely silly eyes of the deer regarded her without fear. It flicked its ears, turned and nibbled at its own coppery flank, turned again its elegant neck, looked at her, and passed on into the woods. Maggie, smiling with pleasure at the sight of the deer, took out of her knapsack some fruit and biscuits, dipped her little plastic cup, drank of the water, and lay down again. Her fingers strayed and found a pine cone, and through her fingers she saw its rich and elegant brownness. Later, when the sun had passed somewhat over, she set up her rod, chose a likely fly, and on a good clear piece of bank cast across the flowing river.

Maggie continued to cast. In the pleasure of casting over this lively stream she forgot – as always when she was fishing – her own existence. Suddenly came a strike, and the line ran out, there was a quick radiance and splashing above the water downstream. At the moment of the strike, Maggie became a co-ordinating creature of wrists and fingers and reel and rod and line and tension and the small trout leaping, darting, leaping. She landed the fish, took out the hook, slipped in her thumb, broke back the small neck, and the leaping rainbow thing was dead. A thought as thin and cruel as a pipefish cut through her mind. The pipefish slid through and away. It would return.

Maggie drew in her line and made some beautiful casts. The line curved shining through the air backward forward backward forward, gaining length, and the fly dropped sweetly. Again she cast and cast. Her exhilaration settled down to the matter of fishing. Then she became aware that the sun had passed over the arc of sky between the mountains. She reeled in her line, gathered up her gear and climbed to the highway.

She walked along the highway, and she walked straight and well and carried her load so lightly that passing cars did not stop for her. The evening grew darker. A plane, full of invisible beings, roared across the patch of sky between the mountains and disappeared to the west. Maggie walked on – cars had headlights now – and her bags had begun to grow heavy long before she saw lights on the right-hand side of the road, country lights among the trees. She approached a row of small cabins, each with its glow over the door, then a little lighted store. She put down her load and went in.

"Good evening," said the fresh-faced young woman behind the counter.

"Have you a cabin?" asked Maggie, hoping.

"Yes," said the young woman, and they went out together.

Maggie lighted her little stove and made her tea. When she had finished her supper she went through the woods, dark now, in the direction of the river noise. She had her flashlight. She found a fallen log and sat down in the dark beside the whitely curling Similkameen River. A sadness fell upon her and the thin cruel thought returned. What dreadful thing had she done to Edward Vardoe. He who had built himself up to satisfaction was humiliated and angry now, and unhappy with a helpless unhappiness that was shocking because he was unprepared. I can't help it, she told herself once again. I betrayed myself and I betrayed Tom and I betrayed Edward Vardoe when I married him. Now I'm almost happy again ... and he was happy because he had no perception – none – and he will never have perception, and now he is unhappy. I didn't judge him, but I am his executioner just the same ... and he has been my executioner for what I did by marrying him. We have been each other's executioners. Now this is the very last time I will think about it, the very last, she said to herself despairingly, it was too dreadful to bear. He is he and I am I. He will never forgive me, and I shall always go unforgiven. But this is the very last of it. God help me. I am humiliated for always by what I did, for marrying him. I won't think of it – there's no good in it – ever . . . if I can. . . . The cruel dangerous thought slid away and played by itself.

Maggie sat there in the dark and she lifted her heart in desolation and in prayer. The west wind blew down the river channel; and the wind, the river, and the quiet sound of the rippling river, a sigh in the pine trees surrounded by stillness, and the stars in the arc of the night sky between the mountains, the scent of the pines, the ancient rocks below and above her, and the pine-made earth, a physical languor, her solitude, her troubled mind, and a lifting of her spirit to God by the river brought tears to her eyes. I am on a margin of life, she thought, and she remembered that twice before in her own life she had known herself to be taken to that margin of a world which was powerful and close.

She rose to her feet, turned, and with her flashlight picked a way through the trees back to her cabin.

For three days Maggie stayed at the Similkameen cabins. She slept long, walked and watched in the woods, and fished the river. Spring was pouring in over the whole countryside, and she knew that she could not stay any longer. She was refreshed now. She turned back on her journey to Hope and then up the Cariboo Highway on her way to Kamloops.

These days had been for Maggie like the respite that perhaps comes to the soul after death. This soul (perhaps, we say) is tired from slavery or from its own folly or just from the journey and from the struggle of departure and arrival, alone, and for a time – or what we used to call time – must stay still, and accustom the ages of the soul, and its multiplied senses, to something new, which is still fondly familiar. So Maggie, after her slavery, and her journey, and her last effort – made alone – stayed still, and accustomed herself to something new which was still fondly familiar to her.

When she took her seat next to the window of the bus leaving Hope, a woman sat down beside her.

Seven

WHEN HILDA SEVERANCE came in from her office she saw her mother sitting behind a cloud of smoke. Mrs. Severance flicked a letter toward her, on the table. Hilda opened it.

"Maggie," she said.

"What address?"

"Just Vancouver."

"What postmark?"

"Vancouver. She says nothing . . . really . . . but . . . she's gone."

"Good," said Mrs. Severance.

Hilda sat down. She read, "It's easier for you both and easier for me if I don't tell you where I've gone. You will understand, perhaps, that my life wasn't endurable. . . . " "That calm placid Maggie!" exclaimed Hilda, looking up at her mother and then continuing to read. "My plans have been made for some time and have been a great support to me. I shall write to you when I am settled, and where, but whatever happens I shall not come back. I'm not asking anything of you, Hilda, unless, if you can help Edward, do. Perhaps you can. I can't. Of course one never expects to arrive at this point in one's life, but here I am. I won't talk about 'feelings.' My love to you both – Maggie."

"D'you suppose she's written to him?" said Mrs. Severance.

Hilda made a gesture that said How do I know?

"D'you intend to tell him you've heard?" asked her mother.

"I think I should but I don't want to get in touch with him. But ... you see," indicating the letter, "she asks me, doesn't she?"

"I'd write," said her mother, relighting from her stub and mumbling a bit. "He's a little stinker, that's what he is but I think you'd better write.... Did you bring the sole? I'll do it in wine," and she got to her feet and walked into the kitchen.

Eight

JOEY THE taxi driver lived with his father and mother and eight brothers and sisters in some rooms behind some rooms behind some rooms upstairs behind the small office on Pender Street which said Universal Taxi on the window.

There was not much light and not much air, and in fact some of the rooms were not entire rooms but had been divided by partitions for purposes of visual privacy. These partitions did not run up as far as the ceiling. They were made of wood and varnished to a light yellowish color which looked sticky but was not. This does not sound very pleasant, especially as other families lived adjacent. Actually it was very pleasant indeed. The family lived in harmony from morning till night and slept in harmony from night till morning. When one of the older boys returned quietly from taking his shift as dispatcher or driver and poked another boy who woke sleepily, got up, pulled on trousers and a sweater and went downstairs to sit by the telephone or to drive, the family did not waken, although the mother never failed to be vaguely aware of what was going on among her children, what with the partitions that did not go up as far as the ceiling.

The father, whose name was Joe or Mr. Quong or Dad, had the kind of benevolent influence that spreads as far as he has jurisdiction, and, by virtue of his character, usually radiates a little farther still. Moreover he was strict. So it was that Joe's word ran throughout these connecting rooms where his children slept, played, studied, and ate, and it flowed up and down the stairs and into the taxi office, and sometimes onto the sidewalk outside the door where he often stood surveying the scene – always changing, always the same – which he knew very well. Here his younger children hopped, skipped, pushed the smallest ones on scooters and tricycles, got in people's way, and were admonished by Joe. Strangers passing the taxi office sometimes felt a faint and memorable pleasure as they saw and recalled again the stout urbane figure of Joe whose white shirt shone below his face of a smooth ivory color. He had, of course, many friends in Chinatown who stopped and chatted. His office was a sort of small and crowded social club where people spent their time talking. Sometimes there was much argument. Some members of the club drifted in and stayed there all day, saying nothing. They then went away somewhere, and no one knew what they thought, if they thought, or where they went, and no one cared. Joe's expression was benevolent, since he was a benevolent man. He was also very sagacious and was not easily deceived. One of his little girls had inherited an ivory skin.

The mother, whose name was Mrs. Quong or Mother, was a small insignificant woman of enormous character. Her children never desired to quarrel among themselves. Whether this was due to the powerful domination of the mother or whether some alchemy in which Joe and the mother had separate parts had wrought this miracle, no one could know, and no one wondered. The result of this was that in the Quongs' home – for these partitioned rooms were indeed a home – there was almost ceaseless noise and clatter, but the noise was not of crying or of anger and nobody minded the noise to which the sound of a radio was usually added.

The family of nine children was a healthy family in spite of all the reasons why they should not be strong and healthy. The youngest little boy was blind, but he was healthy too, and he was so much beloved and watched over by his brothers and sisters that one might say that he was luckier than many other little boys; but that, of course, could hardly be. The children's names were Sam, Alfred, Joey, Yip, Angus, Billy, Greta, Joan, and Maureen. Angus wore spectacles and was short of stature. He admired Joey and wished to be like him, but that was impossible.

As Sam and Alfred grew up and drove the taxis, and now as Joey had begun to drive too, Joe had bought another not very good taxi (that made three in all), and then Yip would soon be able to drive as well. Then there were two cousins nearby. Some horse-riding families make up polo teams among themselves. The Quong family had a taxi team. Joe did not drive and he spent long pleasant idle and busy hours within reach of the telephone and kept a guiding hand on things. Angus was big enough and smart enough to take messages. He was very earnest, and that made him fairly reliable.

Joe spoke both English and Cantonese. Mrs. Quong spoke Cantonese only. She understood English but she did not care for the language so she did not speak it. She got along very well in her own world of her family and friends and neighbors. The children spoke to the mother in either language and did not notice.

It was very pretty to see one of the big boys amble up from where he had parked his car, and walk through a web of little brightly dressed children who usually rushed up and embraced him round the legs. The big boy would pick up a child at random, give it a razoo in the air and set it down squealing for more and would then walk on to the office. Greta, who was sidewalk-broke and had a permanent, was constantly to be seen bending, with her little rump sticking out behind and each curve of her small body instinct with care and preservation, herding Maureen or the blind brother or a neighbor baby away from the curb. That was Greta's function. Maureen had no permanent yet. She was a doll with straight hair and an ivory skin and a face of secrecy. Joan was indistinguishable from anybody else.

Joe's boys had often been approached by dope peddlers and could have made a lot of money in the business, but now the peddlers did not approach them unless they were new to the place. It was well known that Joe would take the hide off of the boys if they had any truck with those peddlers, and, anyway, the boys despised them.

So when Joey came home and told Joe about what the lady had said about partners and the business, they both thought it was pretty funny. When Joe told the mother she said That was an awful woman and not to have anything ever to do with her, out to get young boys like that. But both Joe and Joey said No, she was not that kind of a person at all, she was a lovely woman, but still they couldn't understand it. The rest of the family soon knew about what this character had said, because all the boys had experiences of one kind and another and everything was discussed. The family thought it was pretty funny, and then they forgot all about it.

Nine

M R. SPENCER of Thorpe & Spencer, Sporting Goods, remarked to himself that Mrs. Lloyd hadn't come yesterday. A week later he said irritably "Anybody see Mrs. Lloyd?" and everybody said No.

Mr. Spencer suddenly remembered an unidentified envelope that had come to him through the mail a short time before. Inside it, clipped to a blank sheet of paper were two two-dollar bills, thirty cents in stamps, and a feather. He seemed, now, to see the gray eyes, rimmed with dark lashes, of Mrs. Lloyd, looking at him across the empty envelope.

I shall never see her again, he thought, and discovered that he felt unfairly deprived.

Ten

"I SAW Edward Vardoe today on the way home and I saw him yesterday," said Hilda Severance to her mother. "He looks terrible."

"How d'you mean 'terrible,'" said her mother.

"Well, that jaunty look of his and his face black and pasty." ("How can it be black and pasty," murmured her mother.) "He's going through some kind of a dreadful time. He looks quite wicked. I was frightened of him and I was sorry too."

"Did you speak to him?"

"Me? I? No thank you. I'm not as fond of theater as you are. I put my parcels in the back of the car and drove off. It's really a revelation – Maggie living with anyone who can look like that."

Mrs. Severance's fingers patted the Swamp Angel absently. She was silent for some time. She reached across the table and pulled a writing pad from under the litter of weekly reviews that were her only reading. She lighted a cigarette and did not speak, thinking as she smoked. Hilda went into the garden. When she returned, her mother gave her a stamped envelope.

"Mail this tonight, will you?"

Hilda looked at the envelope and her fine brows went up. "Oh," she said, with her special expression.

On a Friday afternoon Edward Vardoe drove up to Mrs. Severance's house in his new car. The car, it was true, proceeded forward, and within it was the person of Edward Vardoe, but the person within Edward Vardoe retreated backward. He did not wish to go to see Mrs. Severance, but something imperious in her letter had made him leave the office early and go through the mechanical motions that took him like fate to Mrs. Severance's door, which was slightly ajar, and into the room. There she sat in her vast accustomed chair. Edward resented a feeling of being reduced by the large calm presence of Mrs. Severance. His anger, his righteousness, his arguments dispersed and he could do nothing about that. All that was left was self-defense, for and against. For and against what? He looked at her hands which were too small for her.

"How do you do," said Mrs. Severance politely. "How are you?"

"I'm fine," said Edward Vardoe, untruthfully.

"Good. Sit down. Don't put your hat on the table. You can hang it up. Have a cigarette."

"Thanks I don't mind if I do," said Edward Vardoe, jauntily ill at ease. He lighted a cigarette and sat down, bolt upright. He noticed at once the butt of the small revolver protruding from a paper on the table where it lay in its accustomed place.

"I didn't bring you here to talk about *why* this happened and to take sides," said Mrs. Severance gently. "I am very sorry for you but that does not take away my license to be sorry for Maggie whose name we will not mention. I am going to bring you salvation if you want it."

Edward Vardoe stared at her and she saw that his face was pasty and that his brown eyes were dark caverns, so that he was, as Hilda had said, both black and pasty.

"Are you eating well?"

"My stummick's out," mumbled Mr. Vardoe. Mrs. Severance winced and went on.

"Are you sleeping well?"

"Not so good," said Edward Vardoe, with bags under his eyes.

"Do you face the day with a song? I mean how do you feel when you get up in the mornings?"

"Rotten."

"You're drinking more than you did, aren't you?"

"Say, what are you trying to get at!" he cried, jumping to his feet.

"Sit ... down ... " she commanded, and he sat. "Compose yourself, Mr. Vardoe, and I will do you good, but if you don't compose yourself and listen, I shall spend no time on you." (He hasn't much control, has he, she thought.)

He blinked, looking at her, and she narrowed her eyes frighteningly. She blew smoke slowly and contemplated the tip of her cigarette.

"In the evening," said Mrs. Severance, "when you get off the bus or out of your car or whatever it is and go into your house, you don't want to go in. It feels dreadful and I grant you – it is. It looks messy, and it is. You hate eating tinned things. The ashes are cold and days old in the grate ... yes? ... and the house is dead and after a bite to eat you sit down to read the paper and then you have a drink and then you have another but you cannot concentrate on the paper, and you begin your regular evening hate of her. ... " Mrs. Severance dropped her voice and said very softly, "And then you start thinking revenge ... and murder would be a pleasure. ... "

"Oh!" said Edward Vardoe. He clapped a hand to his mouth, but he did not contradict her.

"And then," continued the soft voice of Mrs. Severance, "you have another drink, and you get to *wishing* murder, and if she came in at the door. ... Listen. I know all about you." (She does, thought Edward, with unhappy eyes.) "You're sorry for yourself. ... Be quiet! ... self-pity is dynamite, you should know that at your age. It's ... what? a month and more since she went away. When two months to the day have gone, you must get in touch with my daughter Hilda, and she will come and help you pack every single thing that belongs to your wife. You can store it in our basement, or anywhere you like, or you can give it away, or sell it, or burn it."

"That's right! Burn it!" said Edward Vardoe, leaning forward, seeing the flames licking up and up. "She walked out on me!"

"She forfeited it by going away."

"That's right, that's right, sure, she forfeited it! That's what she did by acting like that! She ... "

"She forfeited it," went on Mrs. Severance, and thought: It was cheap for her at that price. "Then you must empty the house, sell what you want, and keep what you want. I'd keep nothing, if I were you, except your clothes of course. Sell the house. Take a small bright flat – two rooms in the West End. Entertain at dinner once a week."

"Who'll I entertain?" asked Eddie Vardoe. Mrs. Severance found the question shocking in its simplicity and its need.

"Your partner and his wife – hasn't he got a wife? – and some woman friend of theirs. I tell you, Vardoe, if you keep on as you're going now, you'll go down, and out of sight."

Through the turmoil of Eddie's mind the face of Octavius Weller looked at him in a way that made him uneasy, and he knew that what this formidable woman said was true.

"And as to finding her and punishing her, which you know you've thought about, don't be ridiculous. Even killing her wouldn't hurt her ... it would only hurt you ... it wouldn't touch her. She's not that kind. She is punishing herself.... " and Mrs. Severance paused for a long moment. "If," she said slowly, "in a year's time you need to marry again, come and talk to me about it." Edward's spaniel eyes swam with tears but he did not speak. "Now leave me." He stood up. "You should wait out the two months so that you can always say to yourself 'I waited.' But between now and then you'd be wise to pack a bag and go to a hotel, any hotel, a boarding house, it'd be easier for you and you can find a flat and sell your house. Do as you like about that ... and then telephone my daughter in two weeks' time. You've got a new life ahead" (you poor fool, she thought), "if you'll do as I say. Now go. You shouldn't exhaust me like this. I'm old. There's your hat. Don't stand talking. I'm not strong, I tell you. I have to go to bed. All right. All right. Just slam it. It locks."

She heaved herself out of her chair, the powerful willful old woman, and stood at the window watching Edward Vardoe getting into his new car. She smiled a faint smile but her face was not happy because she saw Edward in his helplessness and his meanness and his stupidity and she thought again that life is unfair. "It's not fair ... not fair," she murmured, and then she went into the kitchen and made a tall pot of cocoa. She took the cocoa on a small tray to her bedroom. She put the tray on a table beside her bed and climbed heavily onto the bed. There she settled down, a little tired, and there her daughter found her when she came in.

"Well, Edward Vardoe was putty in the hand," said Mrs. Severance. "He's an unpleasant object but worth salvation I suppose. I quite see it was the only thing that Maggie could do. It's usually compassion of some kind that starts it in a case like that ... I've known it before ... if it weren't for Maggie I wouldn't have touched him ... but I swear to you, Hilda, he was headed for murder if ever he found her. I made a good guess and he gave himself away. It's self-pity, not love, that hurts him. But I opened vistas ... vistas ... " waving her little pointed hands vaguely. "This cocoa's cold ... hot it up or make some fresh." She lighted a fresh cigarette from the stub of the old one. "You can bring me a cup while you're about it. I'm exhausted I tell you. Saving souls. Very tiring." And she settled on her pillows.

Hilda, so slim, so dark, looked at her mother and then she went and made a pot of tea regardless. She loved her mother dearly and hated her a little. People should not be so powerful. People should not always succeed, and so she made tea.

Hilda walked through the parlor and there she saw the handle of the Swamp Angel which lay in its accustomed place. The mood induced in Hilda when she saw her mother toying with the Angel was an emanation from the Angel and from many years. Memory often and often recalled had created for her round the Swamp Angel a mood which resembled memory inasmuch as it drew the past into the present. She could, if she wished, at any moment, see herself clearly at school again where she seemed to have lived throughout so much of her childhood while her parents went to strange places. She was aware of the outline of herself in a uniform from which head and arms and legs protruded, and within which was the person – herself – who looked at the girls whom she saw more clearly in the playground. This child who was herself said a little boastfully, "That's nothing, my mother can do trick juggling with real revolvers on a real stage!"

There was a movement among the girls. "And does your father juggle too?"

"No, my father's not a juggler, he's a gentleman – and my mother doesn't juggle any more – not at the circus. But she juggles."

Hilda saw the look pass from one to another and saw that the boast had tipped over and fallen on the wrong side. She could not tell why. She could see the girls, now, looking at her and talking together. The looks from one to another became smiles, and then "Her mother's a juggler and her father's a gentleman" ... "Did you hear what Hilda Severance said – her mother's on the stage, she juggles revolvers and her father's a gentleman" ... "What did she say? What did she say?" ... "Her mother's a juggler!" ... "Her mother's a *juggler?*" ... "Isn't it a scream, her mother's a juggler!" And the words became her anguish, "Her mother's a juggler!" Everyone seemed to think it was very funny, a joke, a scream, that Hilda Severance's mother should be a juggler and that she had said "My father's a gentleman!" "And she hasn't got a real home!" said the girls. "Hush, dear," said a teacher.

But in the holidays, then she and her father and mother were often together . . . oh in the holidays, what a rushing back, arriving a day or two late, joining the schoolgirl, bringing presents, enameled boxes, a little fan, and – later – pearls; leaving a day or two early, bringing, too, with the mother, an uneasy divided allegiance (there is no more uncomfortable feeling) to Philip who was impatient to be gone, and to Hilda who . . . well, what did Hilda want? She was only a child, and how could they take a child away from school to Troy, to Ravenna (it was important, Philip had said, that they should go to Ravenna). The water was bad to drink; they kept strange company; they lived like vagabonds; there were marshes; it would be unhealthy, quite unsuitable for a child; later, said Philip vaguely. So the mother excused herself to herself but did not convince herself. "Darling," she said uneasily, "we'll soon be back – you'll see – and then we'll have a wonderful time."

"Yes," said Hilda.

But the revolver went everywhere.

There, now, on the table, lay the Swamp Angel, the little survivor of three revolvers, which in her adolescence Hilda had grown to hate. By then the climate of her childhood had become the little-changed climate of her adolescence which now was an east wind in the climate of her womanhood. Something which was both proud and intuitive had prevented her from bursting into hurt and angry disclosure when she saw her mother habitually toying with the Swamp Angel, the little survivor. Her mother would have looked at Hilda in shocked surprise. She would have said nothing and she would have suffered for Hilda, too late, endlessly, all wasted now, and she would – without fuss but with remorse – have put the Angel out of sight. All its pleasure would have perished, and its company, its memory, would have been lost to her. So the Angel had been suffered to remain as the symbol of years of life gone away, and had so remained, and was, thus, Hilda's unique gift to her mother, although her mother did not know that. And now – did Hilda really care much, any more? Perhaps not. Perhaps it was a source of pride that she held this gift voluntarily in an uneasy reserve of which her mother knew nothing. Yet Hilda could not ignore the Swamp Angel which was her mother's habitual companion.

Having made the tea, she went to her mother's bedroom, but Mrs. Severance had gone to sleep.

Eleven

WELL, JUST to think; to have been that boy in the store; and then the young man with fallen arches who could not go to the war; and so to have taken the load off old Macgregor and been, really, the store manager, knowing all the country people, and knowing Mr. Macdonald at the fishing lodge, who was such an educated man, and his daughter, who had gray eyes and cooked and ran the lodge and gave the big orders at the store. Up and up and up, the industrious apprentice. And then, in the tightening of everything as the war went on, the closing and loss of the lodge, and Mr. Macdonald ailing badly. His daughter had married Tom Lloyd who went off as a flyer, and Tom Lloyd was shot down. Things like that were happening all round the countryside, losses and tension. Eddie Vardoe had become pretty bossy and bumptious, people thought, running the store and saying No to people like that. It was too bad, Mrs. Lloyd's little girl died when the polio came, and Mrs. Lloyd went about as if she were made of stone, and then Mr. Macdonald died too. It was very very hard to get help in the store, and Mrs. Lloyd, moving more like a machine than a person, came and worked in the store and Eddie Vardoe was very respectful because she had been Miss Macdonald whose father was such an educated man, and then Mrs. Tom Lloyd. . . .

And now look into this terrible gulf that had opened between the time that Mr. and Mrs. Edward Vardoe were married (to everyone's surprise), and came west – and this very night when Eddie had sat in front of Mrs. Severance, and was now driving home from the show in terrified obedience just as, once, he used to retreat from a tongue-lashing from old Macgregor when he – Eddie Vardoe – was just the boy in the store; poor boy.

Twelve

U P IN the hinterland of the North Thompson River
and far from the ordinary habitations of man was a
place called Table Grande (like grandy). Table Grande
consisted of a small flyblown store, some scattered shacks,
and a name. It had no particular reason for existence. No
one would choose to go to live there, and those who by
misdirected choice had once gone there had not the
energy to leave. It is probably derelict now.

On the outskirts of Table Grande (if Table Grande
could be said to have outskirts) was a group of shacks that
constituted the stump ranch of Mr. and Mrs. Mordy. Mr.
Mordy was lazy and Mrs. Mordy was shrewish. The
stumps that were still left unburned had stood uselessly in
that cumbered stony soil for years; a stringy cow tried to
find sustenance; some stringy fowls ran about; there was a
poor vegetable patch and a root house in which the root
vegetables were kept during the winter. Mrs. Mordy continually nagged at her husband to leave Table Grande and
go to find work in Kamloops, or even in Cottonwood
Flats or Barrière; but every time that Mr. Mordy found
himself faced with moving his wife and two children from
the known discomfort and penury of Table Grande to the
unknown future in Cottonwood Flats or Barrière or Kamloops, he slumped back and said "Aw quit nagging . . . we
got all the winter's wood in haven't we? Wait till spring."

The two children in this family were named Cyril and

Vera. There was no school in Table Grande because there were not enough children to warrant the Provincial Government building a schoolhouse and providing a teacher. There were only the two little boys at the store, and Bill Ford's wife who was going to have a baby any day God help her, and Cyril and Vera Mordy. If Mrs. Mordy had been a different kind of woman she would have written to the Department of Education in Victoria and received lessons by mail. These lessons would have been so well and easily planned that she could have educated Cyril and Vera fairly well; but she did not do this. The result was that Vera educated herself a very little with the help of some old schoolbooks, and that Cyril did not educate himself at all. He was called Surl, and when he had to write his name he spelled it S-u-r-l, so that ultimately he became Surl – Surl Mordy.

Mrs. Mordy did not care for Vera who resembled herself, being slight, pale, dark and thin-faced. She worshiped Surl who resembled in form a Greek god who happened to inhabit western Canada. Surl grew up into undeserved beauty, heroic in form but in nothing else, and crowned with a thick and strong tawny mop of curling hair. There was one thing about his face that was peculiar. His eyelids were set a little low across his eyes, and when he looked at a person, he looked not at the eyes of that person but at that person's lower lids, from under his own lids. This gave his look a slightly sensual yet bashful cast and, later, was a source of excitement to young girls, and older ones too, who saw something personal in this curious regard which did not mean a thing and was simply a physical characteristic. Surl was no good.

This kind of life did not make Vera a happy girl. It is well known that young people need and love love, and Vera did not receive love, unless you could call the lazy tolerance of her father "love." Her mother's partiality for Surl caused Vera's face often to have a bitchy look.

One day Mr. Mordy stood in his shack doorway holding

a sack filled with various objects. The base of the sack rested on the floor.

He said to his wife, "I'm going in to Kamloops. I'll send for you and the kids when I get fixed up with a job of work." He then lifted the sack over his shoulder, turned, and lumbered off to an old jalopy which had stopped first at the store where Mr. Mordy had happened to be that morning. The driver who was a commercial traveler of sorts started up the engine, Mr. Mordy clambered in, and Mrs. Mordy – standing at the shack door – saw the car bump into the distance. She had begun by calling after the car and saying all sorts of things, but that was useless.

Mrs. Mordy and Surl and Vera continued to subsist for some months at Table Grande until, greatly to Mrs. Mordy's surprise, a message really did come from her husband stating that he had a job with the City (it was in the garbage) and that she and the children could now come to Kamloops as soon as they liked. He did not suggest how they should get there.

When they at last arrived at Kamloops, Vera looked at the people and was much ashamed of her ignorance and her shabbiness and not only hers, but of the ignorance and shabbiness of the whole family. She experienced, however, together with this recurring shame, a feeling of strange happiness which was really the feeling of hope and opportunity. The bitchy look was seldom on her face. She watched the other girls and soon became a fair imitation of a nice neat young girl. She presented herself at one of the schools and in an awkward manner told her story and said she needed some education. She was advised very kindly and joined a night-school class which was for the benefit of foreign immigrants who wished to learn to read and write. She progressed fast. She moved on to other classes and before long became a fair imitation of an ordinarily badly educated young girl. Because she was not happy by nature (circumstances had arranged that) she was a little apt to have trifling growing jealousies of other girls, and only policy prevented her from showing the resentments she sometimes felt. She consumed these jealousies in secret, somewhat enjoying them. Otherwise she deserved a great deal of credit. Surl – aided by his phenomenal good looks – took to bad company, narrowly escaped a bit of trouble, and left town. Mr. Mordy was for the first time in his life in a position of some solvency and comfort. He then perversely took pneumonia and died. Vera had inherited her father's weak chest (there was nothing else to inherit) and was subject to colds and bronchitis.

After Mr. Mordy's death Vera and her mother lived uncongenially together but Vera, no longer limited by life on the stump ranch, did not mind. She had a nice job as a waitress in a Greek restaurant on the main street. It was an old-time restaurant run by a Greek called Caesar who was good to his girls. His customers were chiefly ranchers and their families from out of town, commercial travelers and cowboys. Some were rough customers and some were not, but Caesar would take no nonsense for his girls. Later, a friend of Vera's who worked in a large store told her that there was a job going in women's hosiery. Vera, hesitating a little, left the restaurant and took the job.

Since Surl had departed he had written twice to his mother. The second time he gave an address which was the Hotel Del Roxy. This fancy address pleased Mrs. Mordy very much and gave her the idea of going to Vancouver to join Surl at the Hotel Del Roxy. Vera gladly gave her the fare, and Mrs. Mordy set off.

When Mrs. Mordy arrived at the hotel which was a mean-looking joint, she did not seem able to find Surl and it was only by chance that she discovered that he was working as a waiter in the beer parlor. Surl was only moderately pleased to see her. The hotel was in the east end of the city and it is strange to think that Surl had no curiosity about the rest of the city of Vancouver – about its magnificent park, its fine beaches, its pleasant houses, its flourishing businesses both large and small, its elegant suspension bridge, and its mountain trails. The radius of four or five blocks of comparative squalor surrounding the Del Roxy Hotel suited Surl well and he had already formed dubious intimacies and occupations. As far as Mrs. Mordy was concerned, she sometimes sank and sometimes swam in Vancouver, but she did not return to Kamloops.

When the war came there was a shortage of male help everywhere and that included the store where Vera worked. Vera was therefore promoted to the Gents' Furnishings department as the two young gents who usually sold furnishings to other gents had gone to the war. In the evenings, twice a week, Vera went with her best friend to the Services' Club which was run by some hardworking philanthropic and patriotic women on behalf of the men stationed temporarily in and around Kamloops. The club was well run and only girls of good character were permitted to go there and act as hostesses and dancing partners for the men in uniform. It was there that Vera met a man called Haldar Gunnarsen.

Haldar was a good fellow and undoubtedly attractive in his dark way. He had recently been promoted to sergeant, and it was nice for Vera that Sergeant Gunnarsen danced with her, invited her to shows, and at last asked her to marry him. Vera was almost pitifully excited, because Haldar was the first solid man to pay her attention. He became the sole object of her thoughts and hopes. Other people were surprised at Haldar's choice because Vera was not nearly as attractive as many other girls who went to the Services' Club and would gladly have married Sergeant Gunnarsen. It is impossible to know why Haldar asked Vera to marry him. It was partly propinquity no doubt, and partly because one night, under the garish lights outside the Zenith Movie House, Vera had looked up at him with a dog's adoration, and he adopted her, like a dog, that very evening. Once adopted, Haldar was good to her although – on the whole – he was not much interested in women.

Vera hoped never to leave Kamloops. In the nighttime she looked forward to Haldar's return from overseas where "They" would no doubt send him, and planned to make a certain two rooms that she knew of very homey and pleasant. It never entered her mind that anyone – certainly not Haldar who came from the prairies – would ever wish to leave a town and go and live in the back-woods. She had not reckoned with Haldar.

We never really know each other before marriage, do we. How could Vera tell that before ever she had met her husband, a man had taken him fishing on a week-end's leave. They had driven about twenty miles into the hills beyond Kamloops, and then they had walked along a forest trail to a lake which was but little known. The fishing was excellent. The man had said that the lake belonged to old Adams but that old Adams had died and the estate was being settled and the place could be had for a song. He also said he'd kind of like to buy it himself but what would he do with a lake I ask you.

Haldar Gunnarsen on his next short leave went to see the agents for the property and paid a deposit. He called his lake Three Loon Lake because there had been three loons on it when he was up there. He was partial to the loon as a bird. During his years overseas his spare time was to be spent in dreaming of the lake and of the building he would do at the lake. He would someday live there. He really spent more of his spare time in planning about the lake than in thinking about Vera although he was fairly faithful to her.

Haldar's suggestion of marriage ("What say we get married, you and me?") was quickly followed by the wedding because there were rumors that the battalion was about to go overseas. What with the fluster of getting married, which was secondary entirely to the step-up of work in the battalion previous to entraining for the East, Haldar had never even mentioned Three Loon Lake to Vera. This was unintentional but a good thing. It would have been a pity for Vera to spend three and a half years dreading and combatting the idea of moving into the backwoods again; but that was what was lying in wait for her.

When Haldar returned safe home from the war and Vera became Mrs. Gunnarsen in fact, she was filled with happiness. Their association had been brief before; but now, day by day, in becoming settled in their home, they seemed to have a real union and much happy married secret give-and-take of the kind that neither Vera nor Haldar had known before but which had been born of their living together. Vera was elevated in her own esteem when, in speaking to strangers, Haldar referred to his wife as Mrs. Gunnarsen ("Mrs. Gunnarsen and I are going up to the lake." Can this be I?); and she in her turn referred to her husband as Mr. Gunnarsen ("Mr. Gunnarsen can't bear sprouts so I never buy them"). This seemed to establish them soundly. Mrs. Gunnarsen became pregnant. When her boy was born, she thought proudly that he resembled his father, and was glad. A continuing feeling of personal inferiority made her conscious of some social and physical lack and, of course, she was watchful and correct in this. Fortunately for her, Surl and Mrs. Mordy had dropped quite out of her life. She could not have endured their intrusion into the life of Mr. and Mrs. Gunnarsen.

Thirteen

E ARLY ON the day that Maggie Lloyd started up the
Fraser Canyon the weather was lowering; then the
great black clouds withdrew and revealed blue sky
between the mountains. Maggie stood for a few minutes
on the brink of the Fraser River. This formidable river
rushed past the village of Hope at great speed, boiling as it
rushed on. This boiling was strangely maintained in a flat
yellow opaque surface. A sinister thing about this river at
this place and season, Maggie thought, was that for all its
force, it was silent. There was no discernible sound. The
dangerous silent Fraser: the dancing Similkameen River.
Maggie turned away and took her place in the bus.

The woman who sat down beside her said "It's certny a
wonderful day."

Maggie turned to respond. The woman beside her had
wide unblinking china-blue eyes. "My," she said, "I'm
prett' near dead! My mother and her sister-in-law's cousin
had to come up from Vancouver last night of all times and
me getting off to Boston Bar this morning And it isn't as if
I even know her cousin She comes from Buffalo and I
wasn't ever in Buffalo in all my life So I said to my
husband Well I had this all planned before they so much
as thought of coming and Gerty's expecting me and he
said Well I must say the least they could of done was give
a bit of warning and I said Well they gave warning all right
if you can call telephoning in the morning warning I don't

and I said to my husband what I can do I can leave stuff in the house and tomorrow they'll just *haff* to do things for themselves and my husband said Well that's okay by me because his people had been up the week before Seems if you live in a place like Hope people seem to think you have nothing to do but have visitors up from in town and I said to my husband Well I'll be back by supper tomorrow so I just came away and I must say I never did such a thing before You live in Vancouver?" All this was said without a break and Maggie felt sure that there was plenty more.

"No," said Maggie after a moment's hesitation.

"Going up country?" said the woman.

"Yes," said Maggie (what do you suppose? she thought).

"That a fishing pole?"

"Yes."

"You fish? Yourself, I mean?"

"Yes, I love it," said Maggie.

"Well say! I guess your husband fishes?"

Maggie hesitated. "Yes," she said. Dear Tom, casting, perhaps, with a crystal fly for a quick jade fish in some sweet stream of heaven.

"Well," said the woman, "that's one thing I can't take – fishing. If you want to have your home look nice you can't have men clumping in and out with dirty boots on One time my husband brought fish home and I said Well if you want me to cook those fish you can clean them yourself and he did and by the time he finished there was fish all over the house there was scales in the new broadloom and I do declare there was scales in the drapes How he did it I don't know So if he goes fishing now he just cleans his fish in the woodshed and takes and brings them in cleaned in his stocking feet . . . "

Maggie amiably paid her debt to society. "Yes," she said, and "No?" and "Oh!" The stream flowed on.

"You been to Boston Bar?" said the woman, not waiting for an answer. "It's just a small place – railway – Gerty that's my friend her husband works on the railway and it

seems like he always works nights. That's one thing about
my husband he works days I said to Gerty I don't know
how you can take it him working nights and Gerty said it
gets her nervous him always coming in different shifts
And the trains I guess you gotta take your living where
you find it but I always say if you got your interests I got a
broadloom for our living room last Fall and ... " a
thought seemed to call her back.

"There's one thing I *will* say," said the woman, "I did
leave bread and pies and no one can beat my bread and
pies You a cook?"

"Yes."

"Perfessional?"

"Well ... yes ... in a way."

"Going to a job?"

Maggie became deaf. She looked out of the window past
which fled the young green of spring, dark firs, small
waterfalls; then a turn of the road brought near the nar-
rowing Fraser River, noisy here, beating madly against
rock sides. She would see each leaf, each stone, each
brown trunk of a tree, but she would not listen any more.

"Fond of Nature?" said the voice.

Maggie did not turn.

"I said Fond of *Nature*?" persisted the voice.

Maggie turned, but before she could say "Yes, and ... "
the voice continued "I'm crazy about Nature I always was
All our family my brothers and sisters were crazy about
Nature but I guess I was the craziest of the lot If you really
want to see Nature you should go ... "

Oh, thought Maggie wildly, am I to sacrifice the Fraser
Canyon to this? So she broke in and said "I've never been
on this road before so forgive me if I don't talk. . . . I don't
want to miss a single thing ... you understand, don't
you?"

"Why certny," said the china-blue-eyed woman, staring,
offended, "if *that's* the way you feel. I wouldn't dream of
intruding," and she became loudly silent. Twenty minutes
later Maggie turned.

"Look," she said, "that must be Hell's Gate, isn't it?"

"Don't know I'm sure," said the woman, with a genteel smile. Maggie turned back to the window, unabashed.

The woman left the bus at Boston Bar. (Boston Bar, where American miners – the men from Boston, the Bostoné in their Indian name – worked the bar for gold in the late eighteen fifties. And there was China Bar where the Chinese worked the bars – and there were Steamboat and Humbug and Surprise bars, and many others up and down the river – worked, and worked out.) A weather-beaten man of middle age took the seat beside Maggie. The journey continued in silence. The trees retreated, now, from the roadway and the road passed between grassy mounds, rippling flowing, it seemed, out of each other. Above them the pine trees ascended. There came into sight for a moment (like a painted picture on the hill above) four sides of a low weather-stained picket fence surrounding a square. How strange the lonely fence on that wild hillside. It had been white once, and so had the three small wooden crosses within the picket fence. The rolling rippling hillocks at the roadside rose and obliterated the more distant crosses up the hill and the neat humble picket fence that gave the crosses their privacy and the look of respect and care. Men lying in their own bit of soil in that immensity. Maggie quickly saw and as quickly lost sight of the crosses. She turned to the man beside her.

"Do you know this country," she asked, hesitant.

The man pushed back his hat and spoke slowly. "I sure do. I was born and raised up there in Ashcroft and I've spent my time up and down the line."

"Then you can tell me – the three white wooden crosses . . . inside a picket fence? There don't seem to be any people near here?"

"Well," said the man, "I guess there never were. Always some in the hills or somewhere. Not many. Mighta been Indians. Mighta been men working in the old construction days. Couldn't a been folks from real places like

Lytton or Ashcroft because they'd a been taken back there for burial." He said "burr-yal." "Kinda lonely, but kinda nice there."

Yes, thought Maggie, it was lonely but it was nice there. The picket fence and the crosses would be covered by snow in the winter. Then the spring sunshine beating on the hillside would melt the snow, and the snow would run off, and the crosses would stand revealed again. And in the spring the Canada geese would pass in their arrows of flight, honking, honking, high over the silent hillside. Later in the season, when the big white moon was full, coyotes would sing among the hills at night, on and on in the moonlight, stopping, and then all beginning again together. Spring flowers would come – a few – in the coarse grass. Then, in the heat of the summer, bright small snakes and beetles would slip through the grasses, and the crickets would dryly sing. Then the sumac would turn scarlet, and the skeins of wild geese would return in their swift pointed arrows of flight to the south, passing high overhead between the great hills. Their musical cry would drop down into the valley lying in silence. Then would come the snow, and the three wooden crosses would be covered again. It was indeed very nice there.

Suddenly Maggie saw three or four bluebirds, as blue as forget-me-nots in flight. They flew with dipping flight and were out of view. "Oh," she said, "did you see that?"

"Bluebirds?" said the man. "They sure are pretty." The hills fled past.

Soon the man beside her spoke again. "You wouldn't think," he said, diffidently, "that once there was camels treading them mountain sides."

"*Camels!*" exclaimed Maggie. "Not *camels!*"

"My grandfather seen em. He could certify. Smelt em too."

"*Where* did the camels come from? What for?"

"My grandfather never heard where they got the camels. But they figured they'd use em for transport to the gold mines. And they did, for a bit. But them rocks played old nick with the camels' feet and they smelt so high they stampeded the horses and mules every which way. My grandfather said it was fierce. I heard there was one stayed up somewheres near Cache Creek but I never seen it myself. Funny isn't it when you come to think." And it was funny.

Maggie and her neighbor lapsed into silence. Then "Was that sagebrush?" she asked.

"Didn't see it. Mighta been. The sage begins round about here. You'll see plenty that before you get to Kamloops."

Soon the sage began in good earnest, and Maggie saw that the aspect of British Columbia had changed. They were leaving the mountains. Hills and great rocky eminences lay back of the sagebrush. Here and there was an Indian rancheree.

Maggie opened a map upon her knee. What will it mean, all this country? Flowing, melting, rising, obliterating – will it always be the same ... rocks always bare, slopes always bare except for these monumental trees, sagebrush country potential but almost empty, here, except for the sage and the wind flowing through the sage. The very strange beauty of this country through which she passed disturbed Maggie, and projected her vision where her feet could not follow, northward – never southward – but north beyond the Bonaparte, and beyond the Nechako and the Fraser, on and on until she should reach the Nation River and the Parsnip River and the Peace River, the Turnagain and the Liard, and north again to the endless space west of the Mackenzie River, to the Arctic Ocean. What a land. What power these rivers were already yielding, far beyond her sight. Even a map of this country – lines arranged in an arbitrary way on a long rectangular piece of paper – stirs the imagination beyond imagination, she thought, looking at the map, as other lines differently arranged in relation to each other have not the power to stir. Each name on the map says "We reached this point, by broken trail and mountains and water; and when we reached it, thus and thus we named it."

"Coming into Lytton," said the man laconically. Maggie looked up. "There's kind of a nice thing at Lytton people like to see. Like to see it myself . . . ever since I was a kid. Maybe you'd have time if the bus stops for a lunch . . . there's two rivers comes in, there's the Fraser from the north and the Thompson from the east and they're two different colors where they join. Fraser's dirty, Thompson's kind of green blue, nice water. Mightn't be so good now. Depends on how high's the water. Depends on time of year. People tell me there's two great rivers in Europe act like that but I'll bet they're no prettier than the Thompson and the Fraser flowing in together. . . . I'll show you where when we get to Lytton and you can run along down if *he* says there's time. I gotta see the garage man myself."

When the bus drove down the slope into the village of Lytton, and drew up, Maggie made her way along the aisle. She stopped at a seat and looked down. A fair little girl with plaits of flaxen hair standing out on each side of her serious face and a sunny fuzz around her forehead sat there. Her feet did not touch the ground. Her mother sat beside her, next to the window. The child was attentive to a large black cat which was in a basket that took up the whole of her lap. The cat had a narrow red leather collar round its neck and to the collar was attached a leash which the little girl held in her hand as though the cat might at any time wish to jump out of the basket. But the cat only lay blinking, comfortable, half asleep.

Maggie bent down and said to the child "May I stroke your pussy?" at the same time lightly scratching the top of the cat's head. The cat closed its green eyes and gave itself to the caress. The child looked up into Maggie's face and said "Yes you can. She is a very well-disposed cat." Maggie loved the child for saying that her cat was well-disposed, and with a look of great sweetness she smiled down at her.

It had become possible for her to look at a little fair girl without being torn with anguish. The sight of a mother with a little girl, of father with mother with a little girl used to be unendurable. Little by little, and insensibly, her cruel loss and misery had receded within her and lay still, and she was able, now, to look at a child without saying within herself "Polly would have sat just so," "Polly would have skipped and jumped beside me like that little girl," "Polly would have looked up at me like that." She had ceased tormenting herself and being tormented; but, without her knowing it, her look dwelt fondly upon every little fair girl.

For a minute she stroked the head of the well-disposed cat. Maggie and the mother smiled at each other over the child's head, and then Maggie moved on. She walked quickly down to the bridge.

It is true. Say "Lytton Bridge" – and the sight springs clear to the eyes. There is the convergence of the two river valleys and the two rivers. The strong muddy Fraser winds boiling down from the north. The gay blue-green Thompson River foams and dances in from the east. Below the bridge where Maggie stood the two rivers converge in a strong slanting line of pressure and resistance. But it is no good. The Thompson cannot resist, and the powerful inexorable Fraser swallows up the green and the blue and the white and the amethyst. The Thompson River is no more, and the Fraser moves on to the west, swollen, stronger, dangerous, and as sullen as ever. The V at the convergence of the valleys shone green with spring and tamed with cultivation. The Lytton wind blew down the two valleys from all the great sagebrush country beyond. Maggie hurried back up the slope.

"I *suppose*," she said reflectively when the bus had started again, "that you either like this country very much or not at all."

"I guesso," said the man. "When I was a kid nothing would do me but to get out, and the war – the first war – suited me fine. But then when I thought I'd settle in the

city – and I *did* settle in the city kindof, I didn't come to
like it. My brother-in-law, he made good money, was a
book salesman. He'd make as good as thirty dollars a day
and he got me started."

"What did you sell?"

"I reckoned to sell encyclopedias. I could tramp the
streets from morning till nine at night, and sometimes I'd
not make more'n two dollars." (Maggie could see this big
man, diffident, unslick.) "He learned me how and gave
me the line of talk and showed me how to move in for the
kill. My brother-in-law was high pressure and he was
tough even if it was a person's last dollar. Seems to me if
you're going to make a success at book salesman you gotta
have quite a bit of larceny in your blood, city people seem
to have larceny in the blood by nature. I got out and came
back, and I never go out now if I don't have to."

Maggie regarded the sprawling hills across the Thompson River near which ran the road. Sage had taken over.
Solitary pines of great dignity marked the greenish gray
and dun landscape darkly. With massive trunks and sculp-
tured bark, each stood with his daily companion, his
shadow. Across the river such trees as these marched in
thin armies up the runnels of the hills which were
strangely colored in places by outcroppings of rose red
rock. The bus sped on.

Maggie and her companion talked very little. She was
content to look, and he was silent.

"Well, I'll be getting out soon, at Ashcroft," he said at
last, "it's been a pleasure I'm sure."

"Oh," said Maggie quickly, "tell me something before
you go. I don't know anyone in Kamloops . . . can you
tell me . . . I want to know about fishing places . . . who'll
I ask?"

The man's face broke into a remembering smile. "Fishing! There's lots of people you could see for fishing.
There's Doc Andrews or Mr. Robson at the Hotel or old
Henry Corder, you'll see his place on the main street with
kind of a lady's boot over it. Brought it out from Ontario

I guess more'n forty years ago and it'd be old by then. Wimmin haven't worn boots like that for donkey's ears. Calls himself a bootmaker and maybe he is. But he's a cobbler and he knows every fishing place for miles. He'll want to send you up the North Thompson where the Chinese boy has a place on the mountaintop. Or to Paul Lake or to Lac le Jeune. There's lots more. D'you want a good stopping place or to rough it a bit?"

"Tell you the truth," said Maggie, "I want a job."

"What kind of a job?"

"I'm a good cook for a fishing lodge, and I can run a place too. But . . . it sounds funny . . . I'd like a nice place where it's running down a bit and I could take over gradually . . . myself . . . and maybe next year . . . or the year after . . . "

"Well, couldn't say about that . . . but you ask Henry Corder . . . a good lodge cook you say . . . well well, you can pick a job anywhere if you can cook and don't mind work."

"I know you can," said Maggie, "that's why I want it . . . and I like it."

"Tell Henry Corder it was Mike Graham told you. Oh . . . " he began to get up, " . . . and if you want a good eating place go to Caesar the Greek's . . . tell him I told you . . . "

"Just a minute, just a minute . . . I can make fishing flies. Could I sell them in Kamloops?"

"Well, that I couldn't say. Don't use em myself. Henry'll tell you. Good luck."

He went, and turned to wave at Maggie as he left the bus stop. She waved back thinking This feels right, this is the kind of thing I know, it's my kind of place, and she settled herself for the last lap of the journey.

Now she was not so lucky. A man got on at Ashcroft and sat down beside her. He began to talk. She answered briefly. Where you going girlie, he said. Stopping long in Kamloops he said. What say you and me go fishing he said. She turned her face to the window. The man looked at her. He saw the curve of Maggie's averted cheek, of her lips, the sweep of her eyebrow. He pressed his knee against her knee and pressed. You and me could get along pretty good, he said, and "Girlie," he said softly, "I wanna tell you that I haven't one pure thought in my head."

Maggie turned and looked behind her, hardly resting her glance on him. All seats were taken. She saw two men sitting together. She picked up her rod case, got up, and pushed past her companion with some difficulty as the bus rocked along. She bent over the nearer of the two men and said "The person sitting beside me seems to want to sit next the window. Would you very much mind changing places with me?"

The man looked up, surprised, said "Sure," and changed seats with her.

"That feller bothering you?" asked the passenger beside the window, rousing himself from contemplation.

"He would of," said Maggie, "and I don't like being bothered."

"Ah'll say," said the passenger and resumed contemplation.

Maggie passed the rest of the journey in peace, drowsing and waking as the bus drove on. There was sage, sage, sage. Rain was falling. The bus stopped and some of the passengers left. Rain magically released the aromatic scent of the sage, and it filled the air.

Two months later, when summer was full, Maggie wrote to Hilda Severance and told her that she was at a place called Three Loon Lake, nearly twenty-five miles from Kamloops. The lake was about forty-five hundred feet up in the hills, she said.

The letter was signed "Maggie Lloyd." "Oh," said Hilda, " 'Lloyd'! Wasn't that her first husband's name?"

"Then it's final. Excellent," said Mrs. Severance.

Fourteen

I'M FEELING smug today."

"Why are you smug?"

"I believe I've succeeded. I may even have saved lives ... whether that's worth while ... I think so. Alberto saw Vardoe. He was having dinner and dancing at the Panorama. Very pleased with himself. There were four of them. Alberto was funny. I said Who was Vardoe dancing with. He said How do I know, she was scrowny, I do not look twice when they are scrowny, I am too busy ... a tribute to my figure I suppose," Mrs. Severance slumped down comfortably into the big chair. "He said Why did that nice woman marry him. He is very cheap. She was crazy. She couldn't love him. I said No of course she couldn't love him, it was compassion. He said Compassion! Compassion is to sympathize and carry the suitcase and give a drink of brandy but not to marry. What the devil is Compassion to marry anyone for. There is love, and not love. Both of them okay. You know where you are. But this Compassion! Well, I said, he had spaniel eyes, she was sorry for him. Spaniely Eyes! Alberto said. Marry a man for dog's eyes! That's a new one. And anyway he's got them shut all night. ... Alberto is very nice. Why don't you marry him, Hilda? He likes you. He thinks you are very distinguished. We could all live together and have a lot of fun and keep a restaurant, love or not love."

"I don't have to marry him for us to keep a restaurant.

Why don't you marry him yourself? He's your friend, not mine."

Her mother continued, "We could have a restaurant and you could sit up high in a cashier's desk looking handsome and Alberto would be maître d'hôtel and give it style, and I would walk through once an evening in my cape and all the tourists would say Hush, that's the woman Elmer told us about who makes the risotto and can hit a fly at thirty paces. . . . What Vancouver needs is not a hundred thousand dollars advertising for tourist trade. It needs ten plain restaurants with famously good food. It's got nearly everything else . . . too much rain for tourists but you can't change rain by act of parliament. I've often thought . . . "

"You realize, I suppose, that if you walked through a restaurant once a night you'd have to get up out of bed every day and dress yourself."

"Oh . . . oh . . . so I should," said her mother. "No restaurant. Come darling, and kiss me."

Sometimes the power that flowed from Mrs. Severance withdrew, and in these timid withdrawals was manifested a tenderness that seemed to belie her.

"Come," said the mother, holding out her little hands, "my beautiful cross darling. I've seen no one all day but the delivery boy. I need the human touch."

"I won't," said her daughter.

Mrs. Severance put down her hands.

Hilda went over and set her lips to her mother's face. Mrs. Severance then drew back and with the tips of her index fingers followed the winglike lines of her daughter's dark brows. In this creamy box of her brow, the mother thought, she is nearly always unhappy – even now she looks cross and unhappy – why does she hold herself so still, why can't she let down like other people, nice and easy. She kissed her daughter.

"You're right," she said. "Don't marry one of these foreigners. They just care for l'amour and their stomachs. What are you doing tonight. It is Alberto's night off and

he is coming in late and I am making a goulash. I made a
Sacher torte this morning. It's too bad that he likes red
wine and I like white wine because that always means that
we have to have a whole bottle apiece. Well, he brings
both."

"I'm going to the Haida Theatre."

"To the Haida Theatre!" exclaimed her mother, beginning to pull herself up out of the chair, "I'll go! I'll come!
I'll put off Alberto. . . . "

"It's two flights upstairs," said Hilda.

"Blast the Haida Theatre," said Mrs. Severance, letting
herself down again. "Who're you going with? That stick
Cousins?"

"Yes. He's not a stick . . . why do you always say 'stick'!
You've never even seen him!"

"Well . . . 'Albert Cousins'! . . . I shouldn't have said
'stick.' But what a name."

"No you shouldn't have said 'stick,'" said her daughter
shortly.

Mrs. Severance proceeded to talk to Alberto Cosco, a
waiter who was a friend of hers.

"Alberto said 'Yoogle the little gun. I love to see you
yoogling the little gun' . . . but I can't juggle it properly
any more." She took up the Swamp Angel and it slid from
hand to hand, molding and curving – it seemed almost –
like goldbeater's skin in a warm palm. "I'm stiff . . . but
when I think how I used to be able to keep them moving
so fluid and slow – how you had to work to get that tim-
ing! . . . and then the drums beginning, and faster and
faster – all timed – and the drums louder and louder – a
real drum roll . . . and I'd have the three guns going so fast
they dazzled, one behind my back and one under my
elegant long legs (such lovely legs!), and one out as if out
toward the audience and then crack-crack-crack and the
audience going crazy and me bowing and laughing like
anything . . . how I loved it." She put down the Swamp
Angel and lighted a cigarette.

While her mother spoke of her distant triumph, Hilda

idled in her low chair, and her own long shapely legs showed in her attitude the extreme elegance that belongs only to long and shapely legs displayed in the relaxed indifferent grace of repose. Her mind, idling, also, but on two clouds, was aware of her mother recounting the distant triumph of guns and drums and skill and legs and applause and the laughing girl. Only in this did her mother seem old, that she recounted from time to time this triumph of over sixty years gone, just as though her daughter had not heard it before. This legend (which was almost a song) was, together with the Swamp Angel, her only proof of a life which had once been garish and vivid to some girl (could it be that I, sitting heavily here, am that girl?), who had long been fugitive into the past, but not yet gone with all the others of whom there was now no trace nor witness; who (this girl) could be retained and treasured only in the retelling of the scene. Memory alone would not do. Memory would fall into the chasm where lay – perhaps waiting – all things and people gone, and so this girl would cease; therefore Mrs. Severance told the tale, and I, the girl, lived. Each time that Mrs. Severance recalled this scene, it sparkled fresh into her mind and she savored it as one might savor an old wine, fresh at each tasting, sharing it with one who, however, did not so much care for the wine. Yes, Hilda reflected, only in this recounting was there any sign of her mother's age. The physical appearance of Mrs. Severance of heaviness and years was intrinsic, now, in her – was, in fact, Mrs. Severance – and seemed to have nothing to do with age, suiting her perfectly as a medium for the expression of her compassion for the human predicament through which she also had passed, for a certain contempt, and for the entertainment which she derived from her view of the human scene which, from the chair where she habitually sat, was both constricted and universal. She enjoyed her life as an observer. She suffered no longer from the inhibition of beauty. Passion was done. She was not cynical, but she was of ironical and amused habit. She spoke again.

"Hilda," she said, "I often think, sitting here when you're out, I've had everything. All the fun. It's not fair. That, and Philip too ... and now I'm content, and all I need are some cigarettes, and the Angel, and these ... " she riffled the papers, "and good food ... and you, of course."

"In that order?" asked her daughter.

Mrs. Severance was about to laugh and say lightly in her usual way "Yes, in that order," but there was a warning in her daughter's tone.

She said to herself I'm demented. I could say these silly things for forty years, and Philip paid no attention, or he thought I was funny. I was a *belle laide* with a funny tongue, and now I'm a plain fat old woman with a silly tongue – and my poor child all set to be galled so easily.

"I know," she said humbly. "I suppose I show off (why do you take things so seriously, my lamb, you are too earnest, I have told you before, you are far too earnest). I don't know how wise or how unwise I've been. None of us know, do we. But I suspect.... You see, you were born late to me, and your father's life and mine was set in what they call 'a pattern' nowadays – our own ways of talking, and being amused, and paying no attention – and the pattern has stayed. You may have a child, late, and then you will know how hard it is to change, and abandon things, and be wise with a child."

"I shall not have a child," said Hilda.

"Don't say that. How do you know? You will marry someone, or this Cousins. . . . "

"*There*," said Hilda, very angry, standing up. "That's what you do. You say that kind of thing. You say a little thing like 'this Cousins,' and all the time perhaps I shall marry Albert Cousins – yes, I say – Albert Cousins. Why is 'Albert Cousins' funny and 'Alberto Cosco' not funny? You have set up a feeling about him between you and me the very way you always say his name. Mother, you are so used to playing God and playing so cleverly that you make gross mistakes. . . . I know, you did well with Edward Vardoe, very well . . . and it's gone to your head."

Her mother gazing fixedly at the ashtray, flipped off the ash of her cigarette and flipped again. Then she looked up and in her tender voice she said "Forgive me . . . my darling . . . for a woman who thinks she is so wise I can be very stupid," and she got up and went into the kitchen and shut the door. Even now, see! thought Hilda, she frustrates me; she just goes away.

Hilda was putting on her coat when she looked up and saw her mother standing there.

"Are you going to get that week off?" asked her mother in her ordinary voice.

"I think so."

"Good . . . " and she turned to go.

Hilda felt the needle of compunction. "If I do, I shall take the car and go on the Island," she said. And then – was there a pause? yes there was – "Would you like to come?"

Mrs. Severance's heart lifted within her. "Thank you darling, no. It would be all scenery, wouldn't it. I don't enjoy drooling over scenery or listening to drooling – 'Oh look at the mountains! How sweet the clouds! Behold the cow!' And I'm too unwieldy to sit in that little bathtub of a car all day – no thank you. But I do adore being asked. I like it best here. Would you take Margaret if she could get away?"

"I might," said Hilda, relieved. "I shall get the Spink to sleep here and do the cleaning and . . . "

"Certainly not. I'm very much attached to Mrs. Spink but she breathes too loud and talks too much . . . for a whole week. Alberto shall leave his room and come and stay. We shall look after each other. He suits me. We shall drink too much wine and I shall have gout in my fingers again. Good night my lamb, in case I've gone to bed when you come in."

Fifteen

As you drive up the winding ascent into the hills behind Kamloops, past the Iron Mask mine, and on, the driver does not look down, but the passenger looks down, and still further down, and toward the beautiful confluence of the North Thompson and South Thompson Rivers which are fluid monuments to the great explorer's name. At Kamloops the rivers join and become the Thompson River which flows westward between the sagebrush hills, spreads into a wide lake, narrows, and races on. The first Fort Kamloops was built at the vantage ground of the junction of the rivers. Kamloops is the Meeting of the Waters.

About twenty-five miles from the town of Kamloops, following a progressively worse road into the hills, is Three Loon Lake. Between Kamloops and Three Loon Lake – which is one of several scattered lakes among the hills – folds of the high land rising and falling away disclose occasional ranch buildings. Some cattle graze and some sheep, domestically incongruous in these hills. For the last five miles, as the road becomes a rocky trail, taxing the driver, there is no habitation. Yet, by the standards of that country, Three Loon Lake is not far from town.

For the last five miles, you drive among trees. The higher sage hills are, by some authority of nature, clothed with spruce and aspen and lodgepole pines. You cannot see a gleam, even, of the water of the lake until you are nearing the lodge. But, as soon as you hear the occasional wild and lonely cry of the loon clattering through the trees, you know that you are near some water.

These lakes lie like giant dew ponds in depressions at the summits of the hills. The ground rises slightly round them, and, if the hill is high enough, the lake is always rimmed with pine forest, very dark and close. In certain parts of the lake shore there is tulé grass growing out into the water, thick at the shore, thin and sparse as it stretches into the lake. Where the tulé grass – which is a tall reedlike grass – is sparse, its angled reflections fall into the water and form engaging patterns. Where the tulé grass is dense, Canada geese may make their nests and lie there with their young, but, more often, smaller water birds nest there and the geese go farther north. Fish feed in the tulé and are fairly safe. Perhaps they become bold, and some acquired knowledge tells them that the fisherman cannot cast into the dense part of the tulé grass. But he casts into the edge of the grass, where a dimple reports that a fish is feeding. The lake gets its name, of course, from the loons who own the lake and have always owned it. There is a mother, large and handsome, and her two lordly children who swim one on each side of her. When they are big enough, she leaves them sometimes and flies high, circling higher, and is joined by another loon from somewhere else. He may be her consort; or perhaps another mother loon has come to her lake. They fly together, and then the visiting loon returns home. The mother swims with her two big babies and sometimes she utters her loud vacuous clattering cry. Is it a laugh? Is it a cry? It is melancholy, particularly at nightfall. It belongs completely to the lake and is part of these regions. It epitomizes the place. All the creatures on the lake hear it. What does it mean? The shores echo the cry back across the lake, and the loon cries again and the echoes clatter again and then silence closes over as always.

Sometimes the fish osprey cruises above. He has a nest at the top of a high tree at the far end of the lake. He cruises and cruises. Then suddenly he drops. He hits the water hard in flying spray. He rises and shakes himself like a dog and the spray flies in a fountain on the still lake. He rises into the sky. In his talons he carries a fish that looks silver in the sunlight. It is a rainbow trout. He does not carry the fish at right angles to his body. His talons hold the trout parallel under his body, and so he rises unimpeded and rapidly and moves off toward his home, looking like a bird with one slim shining pontoon suspended underneath him. Sometimes the loon seems to warn the creatures of the lake that the osprey is coming, for he is a great hunter. He has to be. Sometimes he comes in silence.

When the naked lake is placid beneath the sky, the Kamloops – or rainbow – trout leap and leap. That does not mean that they will take the fly. It may mean that they are lousy, or perhaps they leap for joy. It must be great fun, leaping straight up from water into air, propelled by those small strong smooth muscles – two, three feet or more above the lake – and falling again. In the evening, when the sky and the water are shot with tender colors which grow more violent in lake and sky, this leaping is beautiful to see, here, there, there, near at hand, and diminished across the water. You hear the delayed plop of the leaping fish. Little fountains are everywhere on the lake. One at a time – no – two, three, four. It exasperates, at last, because the leaping fish has no intention of taking the fly. It is when he weaves – bold, timid, swift, secret, hidden – through the opaque waters, or when he is feeding at the edge of the weeds or in some fine undisclosed rich place that he will, perhaps, try the fly, either from hunger, curiosity, or some other fishy attribute of which we know nothing. At Three Loon Lake the water is nearly always very cold, and the fish are lively, striking and running, like whiplashes; the fisherman must play strongly and delicately, for the fish is never his until it lies in his net, impotent.

On the edge of Three Loon Lake Haldar Gunnarsen had cleared land and built, in the Scandinavian fashion and also in the fashion of the Western interior country, a rather large log cabin with eating place, kitchen, a small bedroom for his wife and himself, a cubbyhole for his son, and a storeroom. There was, of course, a stove in the kitchen, and there was also an iron stove of the kind called an airtight heater in the eating room which was a living room for guests if they had any. He added a plank veranda to the front of the lodge and an extension of the cedar shake roof, supported by lodgepoles over the veranda. There were two privies at the back. Then he built five very small log cabins among the trees, each with a stove. He would build a smokehouse when he could afford it. He had, at first, another returned man to help him for a while, and two neighbors who lived some miles away and had a buzz saw helped him too. He used his gratuity money after the war. The wood cost him nothing, except some labor and some planking for the floors. He had to buy nails, stoves, windows, and cement for chimneys and chinking. How he grudged the money for beds and blankets and tin washbasins and many more things which, to his surprise, he found to be necessary – and boats, of course.

His wife was nearly as much interested as he was, but not quite. She was restive, discontented. However, looking forward, she was able to see a row of nice cabins, a better car to make deliveries easier, an improved road, and kitchen help, money in the bank and retirement. She was not quite sure that she wanted her little boy Alan to grow tied up, as it were, to the country, but she knew that you can't have everything the way you want it, and if Alan grew up to be as good a man as his father Haldar, her heart and her head told her that she should be satisfied; yet she was not. However, at first her mind jumped the next few years, and saw the lodge at Three Loon Lake as well known, filled, and famous to the far parts of the continent. Americans from California, New York, Honolulu come for the fishing to remote points of British

Columbia, so she was right to be hopeful. Canadians come from all over the West.

There was, in Kamloops, this man called Henry Corder who knew Haldar Gunnarsen very well. Henry Corder knew every fishing place in the region, and the owners, and the fishing, and the kind of place that would suit the inquiring visitor. He could sum you up as he sat at his bench, and knew how much roughing-it you could take or whether you wanted tablecloths and indoor plumbing. He also knew the kind of fishing you would get at these places and whether, at that very moment, the fishing was good there. He was honest. He did this for love, although some benefits accrued, because he had the gift and the passion. Everyone deferred to Henry Corder. He liked Haldar Gunnarsen very much and encouraged him in his venture. He could not see why Haldar's lodge at Three Loon should not, in a few years, have as fine and justified a reputation as any lodge in the district.

It was therefore a keen disappointment to Henry Corder and to many other people when, the summer after a promising but incomplete first season, Haldar Gunnarsen's car slid in the gumbo off the trail in one of the bad spots about six miles from his lodge, and he was pinned beneath the car. Some fishermen driving in that evening found him. Haldar was alive but his hip was broken and he had other injuries of various kinds. The car was salvaged. That was in the middle of the first full season. Mrs. Gunnarsen and the child Alan closed up the lodge and came down to Kamloops. After eight months in the hospital, Haldar began to move about a bit. While he had lain in the hospital, and, partly in order to divert his mind from severe physical pain, he had planned his next season, and the next season after that. He was undefeatable (he thought), and as time went on he communicated with a man whom he knew, and liked moderately well, who might find it worth his while to see him through the next season, and then, of course, Haldar would be all right. He did not wish to do this, as he had a fiercely possessive feeling for Three Loon Lake, and did not really want this man to have any part in it. But the poor, who also meet with misfortune, cannot always choose. So, as Haldar did not at any time consider pulling out of Three Loon Lake, he had to compromise. Things were made still more difficult for him as his hip did not knit well. He suffered, daily and nightly, a good deal of pain, but, as he was a philosopher, he disdained the pain and attempted to ignore it. He refused to recognize the fact that he would not be of much use at the lodge.

His wife conceived a strong dislike for Three Loon Lake, and wished Haldar to sell it. This she urged him to do as soon as she thought he was well enough to be faced with her strong feelings on the subject. A difference of opinion grew to a bickering and then the subject was closed. Haldar persisted in regarding his crippled condition as a temporary affair and irrelevant, and the lodge at the lake as being intrinsically established and permanent. His judgment had become impaired to the extent that he thought that his wife was unreasonable, and he did not see, or know, that below her argument was a growing fear and dislike of the future with a crippled man and a child at Three Loon Lake. She developed a jealousy against the lake as against a person. He did not even know that he would be a care to her. He regarded himself as a strong man, but temporarily a little lame. There were several reasons that bound Haldar Gunnarsen to Three Loon Lake and it was remarkable that these binding attachments had grown so fast, but land can do that. The land was his, and had at once assumed the character of having been intrinsically his, always, waiting only, ever since lake and shore were made, for Haldar. The place was his future, and he had never had a future, only an imperative present. The character of the place was so much the character of Haldar that he conceived of it as being almost sentient, waiting for him, and that it would wait for his son. This waiting feeling was intensified by the nights and the days that he spent in the hospital when, tirelessly, he roamed Three Loon Lake, and knew that it was his, water and shore.

None of these reasons, or passions, bound Mrs. Gunnarsen to Three Loon Lake. She blamed the place for her husband's disability and accumulated within herself other reasons why she did not wish to see it again. By May, however, the Gunnarsens and a man called Chuffey, together with further supplies for which Haldar had to raise a loan, were at the lake again. They began once more, and a few fishermen came, recommended by Henry Corder. The lodge was not well run, and the cabins were not very clean. Mrs. Gunnarsen was not efficient and had too much to do. Chuffey was lazy, talkative, irresponsible about money, and had a large appetite. Haldar Gunnarsen, in his effort not to show that he suffered pain, was morose, and he worked far too hard, moving slowly in a manner that was painful to witness. Their little boy became bad-tempered because people had no time for him, but he carried the firewood to the cabins and saw that the boats were really tied up, and he helped to hang out the washing, a job which he despised.

They closed the season early, and after trouble with Chuffey, the Gunnarsens found that with all their labor, and his pain, and her resentment, they had ended the year with reduced debt as far as the lodge was concerned. But still there was debt and no money anywhere. Mrs. Gunnarsen worked in Kamloops during the winter and Haldar had a small sedentary job. What a change this was from the fine couple of two years ago, Gunnarsen so strong and light-hearted, and Mrs. Gunnarsen moderately happy although she rather preferred to be unhappy, and now there was something between them that could not be resolved, and they were resentful with each other and with all circumstances, and poverty looked steadily at them through the window, and all on account of six inches of mud.

All winter Haldar made plans for the next season.

"Oh," his wife cried aloud when she was alone in the room, "he is crazy! He's mad! Whatever can we do!" The continued conflict was painful to Mrs. Gunnarsen. That hidden sweetness of marriage which reveals itself between two people in the common ways of touch and sight and peculiar word had gone into a past which could not refresh them. They no longer knew the happy gestures of love; they were too anxious. But she could never never leave him and she would do what he wished, although she would spoil things by doing it grudgingly. Living with her could hardly be called a pleasure.

As spring drew near Haldar Gunnarsen's condition made him unwillingly aware that he was hoping like a fool. But he said to himself "Once up there . . . you'll see . . . " and he still prepared to go, with the first misgivings untold. He had taken the future for granted, and he now realized that all he had been taking for granted was hope.

It was that spring, just after the Gunnarsens had been driven up to Three Loon Lake that Maggie Lloyd arrived in Kamloops and went to talk to old Henry Corder.

When Maggie went up to Three Loon Lake with her knapsack and her canvas bag and her rod and the little yellow bowl which was now her household god, and a large order of foodstuffs that were essential to her cooking (bought and paid for), and all her strength and gentleness and good will, Henry Corder said to everyone who came into the store, "Say! Whaddaya know! . . . I wish to tell you there's some justice! . . . "

Sixteen

I T WAS a fine morning – the whole season was fine, one
day like another – when the Carruthers men brought
Maggie to Three Loon Lake with the weekly supplies, on
their way to their ranch five miles further in. Henry
Corder had forwarded a grapevine message to Haldar
Gunnarsen that he was sending in a woman who'd suit
them dandy. He would come up in about a fortnight
himself, and he bet the man he gave the message to, who
was to give the message to another man if he just happened to see him – he bet that this lady who was a cracker-
jack would fit right in and take a hold of things and the
Gunnarsens would get a break at last. And what's more
I'm telling you, I got that much confidence in her that I'm
sending them three doctors I know from Vancouver ast
me where to go next weekend and her no chance to get the
layout yet, she's not a no-vice, she'll take em in her stride.
The message reached the Gunnarsens in pretty much the
form in which it was sent, and Mrs. Gunnarsen, lifted
from the apathy which had spread from her to the detri-
ment of her husband and child, gave the kitchen a clean-
out, so as to make a fair impression on the newcomer. She
was almost happy. Her load seemed for a time to slide
away. Only a woman who pulls too heavy a load for her
strength and skill could know Mrs. Gunnarsen's emotion.
Not even a horse.

Haldar Gunnarsen received the message with some

relief. Behind his relief was the entrenched feeling that he and Vera could have managed this alone if Vera hadn't behaved the way she behaved, and if he just hadn't had this bad spell. Henry Corder had said nothing about wages for this high-priced character, and Haldar bet himself that when she saw the setup, she wouldn't stay. Little Alan Gunnarsen did not mind one way or another.

Haldar, sweeping out the house slowly and painfully, stopped, and looked toward the trail which emerged from the trees. He heard a car. It might be the Carruthers' truck. "Vera," he called.

The little truck rocked and bounced out of the rough forest road into the sunshine. A woman sat between the two Carruthers men. All three got down from the truck. The woman wore a sweater and skirt and a dark raincoat. Her short curly hair was blown. She stood and looked about her. Haldar liked her looks. He thought she seemed strong and plain and sensible. Vera Gunnarsen had a feeling that the woman was beautiful. The woman turned toward them with a smile.

She bent to her small baggage and then came forward. The Carruthers men carried the cartons of weekly supplies to the kitchen door, stopped for a few words and departed, turning the truck and clattering away into the forest.

Maggie and the Gunnarsens shook hands. Maggie smiled at the little boy Alan and then shook his hand too. Alan looked up at her.

"I'll show you your cabin, Mrs. Lloyd," said Vera Gunnarsen. "It's a bit rough," she said deprecatingly, "but I guess Henry Corder told you. . . . "

"I lived like this most of my life, and this is what I like," said Maggie. "I'll go and change if you'll show me – and I'll come back and we can talk . . . and you'll tell me," she added.

As she moved away to go with Vera Gunnarsen to the cabin, she turned again, and stood. Her look traveled over Three Loon Lake, sparkling, shimmering, melting, silent –

over the lodgepine shores, over the low curves of the hills, knowledgeably to the little dock with the boats, over the log house and the small littered log cabins under the trees.

"Your place is grand, Mr. Gunnarsen," she said. "We think so," he said, and then thought My, she's a lovely-looking woman! The women went on and Alan trailed them. Haldar resumed his slow sweeping. My *God*, wouldn't it be a break! If we could swing it! If she'll stay! If she's really any good! Why ever would she come here! If she doesn't want the earth!

A first meeting. A meeting in the desert, a meeting at sea, meeting in the city, meeting at night, meeting at a grave, meeting in the sunshine beside the forest, beside water. Human beings meet, yet the meetings are not the same. Meeting partakes in its very essence not only of the persons but of the place of meeting. And that essence of place remains, and colors, faintly, the association, perhaps forever.

Seventeen

W ELL," SAID Hilda to her mother, "have you made arrangements with Alberto? Can he come? I'll have to empty a drawer and the cupboard for him in my room, hang him. I really *do* wish, Mother, that you'd have Mrs. Spink. She's not so much fun, I know, but her breathing won't kill you."

"I'd rather have Alberto," said Mrs. Severance.

"Very well," and Hilda turned to go, then quickly turned again. She was suspicious of something in the air. "You *have* arranged with him?"

"I shall telephone him," said Mrs. Severance evasively.

"You telephoned him yesterday!"

"Yes, but he had a very 'leetle' cold. It will be better."

"Really Mother, you are aggravating! Do you think I can go away with a free mind with you nursing Alberto with a leetle cold? He'd adore it. You'd be bending over Alberto's bed all day and him rolling his eyes up and blessing you and you working like a horse and living on the telephone explaining to the hotel that Mr. Cosco has a temperature. I shall telephone him myself."

Mrs. Severance was delighted at Hilda's concern about her, but did not say so.

Hilda spent some time at the telephone while Mrs. Severance sat still, looking amused.

"Your friend Alberto has a bad septic throat. His land-lady seemed to think that he intended to come here just

the same. I think she was disappointed. . . . Mrs. Spink
will come and get dinner and stay and sleep here and get
breakfast and clean up and then go to her family every
day and come back again. It won't be long and I'll be
satisfied."

"Well . . . Really . . . " said Mrs. Severance who was
both chagrined and pleased. She found Alberto amusing,
and was sorry that he had a septic throat. She found Mrs.
Spink diverting, but she preferred her own company and
complete freedom in her small house to Mrs. Spink.

How I love Alberto, she thought. How inordinately he
laughs! He laughs with his hair and his eyes and his teeth
and his fists and his elbows. He shakes this house up like a
cocktail. What the devil does he mean by having a septic
throat. She resigned herself, and prepared a welcome
(*deuxième classe*) for Mrs. Spink.

"Can you be trusted?" asked Hilda, carrying a small
suitcase and a coat and a picnic basket through the room.
"Mrs. Spink doesn't need any cupboards and drawers.
She's not like Alberto. She can change the bed, too."

"Yes, dear," said Mrs. Severance primly.

She pulled herself up from the chair, walked out to the
small veranda and watched Hilda putting the suitcase and
the basket into the back of the absurd car, something like
a bathtub, as Mrs. Severance had said.

Hilda ran up the steps and kissed her mother good-by.
As Mrs. Severance watched her going back to the car, she
beheld her with new eyes. Not the customary Hilda coming in, but the traveler in a small clean car from – where?
San Francisco perhaps? Toronto perhaps? She is very
smart in that flannel suit, thought her mother. It's quite
perfect. Hilda's face that could so easily storm over ("the
black dog on her face," Philip used to say when she was a
child) was glowing. She would pick up her friend Margaret. She started the car, leaned out and waved to her
mother, with the flash of a smile, and was away.

Mrs. Severance watched the little car until it vanished.
She stood with her hands in her dressing-gown pockets. In

one pocket was a packet of cigarettes, some matches, and a man's handkerchief; in the other pocket was the little Swamp Angel which she fingered as she looked about her. The air was cool, nearly cold, fresh after rain. She turned back into the house, walked slowly about, and very much enjoyed an emptiness and freedom that seemed to be there.

The house was ugly and cramped and had been rushed up about fifteen years before. Its front was a botch of small pretentious and superfluous gables and fancy roof. The windows were both too plain and too fancy. A short flight of steps led up to a veranda almost too small for a chair but large enough to say good-by upon. A window looked partly onto the veranda, so that a person standing on the veranda, to the left of the door, could look into the room which Mrs. Severance chose to call the parlor, toward the fireplace which was on an outside wall. At night soft yellow curtains, drawn, gave a look of intimacy, even charm, to the objectionable little house on the thirty-foot lot. Mrs. Severance no longer observed the outside appearance of her house which had long been simply the structure that contained her chair, her table, her bed, and her kitchen.

I will go out, she thought. It's quite nice to be alone. I don't really care for humanity . . . it gets between me and my desires which are very simple, but constant. I think that Hilda thinks I'm "peculiar." Well, perhaps I am. And so, by revulsion, I have made her more conventional, and now she's afraid of what the sight of me might do to this young man, and the other young men. (Mrs. Severance felt wounded, and yet she saw the reasonableness of this.) . . . Well, I can't take to going out in coats and skirts and hats, even to oblige, and she fingered the Swamp Angel in her dressing-gown pocket absently. When Philip was alive we didn't seem peculiar, he and I, not to ourselves anyway. I suppose we lived in peculiar places. I'll brush my hair and put on my cape over this, and go to the end of the block and back. She used the old-fashioned phrase "to take the air." She thought It is a long time since I've taken the air.

She brushed back her coarse gray hair and put on the long cape over her dressing gown. She took her heavy walking stick and went slowly down the steps. She felt that she had made every concession to what was correct, in order not to shame or annoy the absent Hilda.

A woman looking out between the curtains of the next house said "Oh come quick! Look, there's that woman again! Isn't she peculiar!"

Mrs. Severance, not feeling peculiar, walked slowly with much dignity along the sidewalk, looking about her but thinking of Albert Cousins. Her ingenious mind reached out this way and that. She wished to decoy Albert Cousins, and to convey innocently to him that nothing would induce her ever to live with a married daughter, nothing in the world, neither politeness nor persuasion. There are times (she knew) when things should be left alone, but still she thought about the absent unknown Albert Cousins and was aware of her chance.

Having reached the corner, she turned, and walked slowly back to the house. This is very pleasant, she thought, I must do this again. She then took a false step as she approached her gate, and fell heavily to the ground.

Eighteen

O N THE evening of her fall, Mrs. Severance lay in her huge bed with a strapped and aching ankle. Both her body and her mind were tired and sedated. She thought, and then her thoughts slid away. Then she awoke and thought again. Visions, with words, arose which had long occupied her mind; she had not cared to talk about them, except, as now, to herself.

All this nowadays of symbol symbol symból . . . destroying reality . . . too much power, people worship symbol . . . obscures something . . . what . . . obscures . . . she drifted.

She woke. A shade that was Philip passed, and passed again. Where are we Philip, the storm came in bumps. She opened her eyes and saw her bedroom. She closed her eyes again . . . the Angel. The Angel must go . . . because it is a symbol and too dear . . . and some other reason . . . what other reason . . . she drifted.

In that terrible minute this afternoon when she had fallen, she had been helpless and – what was, for her, far far worse – she had lain exposed in her bulk and disarray to the gaze of a gathering crowd of (she thought) youths and a man, some women, children, who had helped and pulled and talked, and not helped and stood and talked, outside her house and inside her house. She who was private had lost all privacy; she and her house had been exposed to curious eyes. The terror was not in the fall, but in that instant when she had heard the word "gun!" and had opened her eyes and had seen the Swamp Angel sprung from her loose pocket and lying just beyond her reach. She had with exquisite pain heaved herself toward the Angel and had grasped it before a rush of two boys descended. If it had been my bag, she said to herself, or my purse, anything but the Angel, I shouldn't have minded. What's a fall? Nothing. The poor old woman! She fell! Thank you, my dear, you're very kind. Does it hurt, now? There then. The Angel was a gun. She had almost forgotten that the Angel was a gun, and therein lay some strange difference to the people at the gate. "Gosh it's a gun! . . . She's got a gun! . . . pleece will . . . better report it . . . registered firearms . . . see, she's hid it . . . I seen it . . . it was laying right there . . . what's she doing with a gun? . . . Lady, was that a gun? . . . Maybe someone's shot her. . . . Maybe she shot somebody . . . "

Mrs. Severance pressed the hard shape of the revolver against her great thigh within the bed. It was not safe beyond her hand. She thought It will live longer than I shall . . . what will happen to it . . . I shall not keep the Swamp Angel any more . . . what shall I do? She drifted away.

She woke again. Through her numbed and dreamy state she heard, not three yards from her closed bedroom door, the shrill of voice of Mrs. Spink who was obeying instructions.

"I couldn't say, I'm shaw," said Mrs. Spink.

. . .   . . .

"I reelly couldn't say."

. . .   . . .

"Mrs. Severing is laying in her bed very sick. She might of broke her ankle. She had a Fall!" Mrs. Spink magnified the word until it nearly caught up with the fact.

. . .   .

"No, you couldn't. The doctor said. The doctor wouldn't allow. Not under any circumstances he wouldn't allow."

. . .   . . .

"I don't know nothing . . . I just work here . . . couldn't say, I'm shaw." This went on for some time.

Mrs. Severance heard the front door close. Printed words in an evening paper swam before her eyes.

"Aged woman wields gun," "presence of revolver unexplained," "understood police will investigate." She groaned.

Poor Hilda. How she would hate this. She was aware that Hilda, for some reason, had never seemed to like the Swamp Angel. And Mrs. Severance, lying there, thought with anguish of the little gun that lay against her thigh, given to strangers, descending to a junk shop, bought by . . . I shall lose it and save it, she thought foggily. I shall feel clearer in the morning. And she slept.

In the morning she ached, and her ankle gave her pain, but she was in better humor. She pulled herself up in bed.

"Bring me that square rosewood box, the little desk," she said.

"There was a young man last night but he didn't get anything out of *me*. I told him to lay off. I said I didn't know nothing. . . . I said to him . . . "

"Yes," said Mrs. Severance soothingly. "You were so good, Mrs. Spink. You were wonderful! I heard you . . . " she was looking at some large sheets of writing paper. She held them to the light. "Get me two slices of dry bread. And the telephone book."

"Bread?"

"Yes, dry bread. And there'll be a box or two in the broom cupboard . . . there's a cardboard shoe box, I think. Bring the box, and some strong paper and string."

"Okay," said Mrs. Spink, thinking Dry Bread?

Mrs. Severance examined and compared a few sheets of heavy cream writing paper. The writing paper bore a crest. She made pellets of the bread and cleaned the paper thoroughly. She had kept these sheets of paper in the rosewood box – why, she did not know – after a visit to the only relatives of Philip's who had accepted and loved her –

long since dead. She must be sparing of this paper which now, she thought, smiling a little, was to be an oblation to snobbery. Whose snobbery? Well, mine, at least, she admitted to herself.

She wrote a rough copy, and studied what she had written, smoking. In her fine large hand she transcribed what she had written onto the ancient paper, fulfilling itself, this September morning half a century on.

My Dear Mr. Cousins

    I apologize for what is really an intrusion. I am in some difficulty, owing to a fall which I had yesterday. Hilda is away, I am almost glad to say, and of my two other close friends one is in the upper country and one is ill. I find myself in need of advice and I am turning to you, as one of Hilda's friends, to help me.

    I am, as perhaps Hilda has told you, rather a recluse. But it would be a great kindness if, this afternoon, you can visit me for a few minutes. I shall not keep you long.

Sincerely
Nell Severance

Mrs. Severance read and reread her note with a half smile. She was now on familiar and pleasant ground. He will be enticed, she said, with her usual satisfaction, and I shall further entice him. Some of the nightmare of yesterday was dissipated. The throbbing ankle remained. But when the mind is made up, and a way opens, how great is the solace. The large elegant hand and the cream and crested writing paper had authority, and impressed even Mrs. Severance favorably. She turned the pages of the telephone book. Then she addressed the large square envelope, crested also:

    Albert Cousins, Esq.,
      Cousins & Son,
        Printers & Lithographers.

The small jubilation which Mrs. Severance felt at the sight of the envelope then departed. In its place came a pang at what she was now about to do. She despised sentiment so much that, as she wrapped the Angel first in one layer of paper and then in another in order that the Angel should not be jolted this way or that in the shoe box on its journey up the Fraser River Canyon, she firmly repressed the grief that she felt rising like a storm at sea. Her grief involved the whole of her seventy-eight years gone, and Philip, and the very form and substance of the Swamp Angel, and not just this moment in time. She wanted to weep as she wrapped the Angel and closed the lid over the shoe box, but she was aware that tears do not become the old. However old a woman may be, or plain, or – as they say – washed out, something that is not exactly pride (although akin to it) but the accumulation of experiences and the knowledge that tears are not seemly in the old discourages the luxury of weeping. So Mrs. Severance did not dramatize the action of tying up the revolver in the shoe box although it was – to tell the truth – the only dramatic action of her life since the year before Philip's death. The little dramas that she had played, sitting there in her chair, for years enough, now, had not sprung from any inner need but from the interested occupation of her amused intelligence. The play that she might play this afternoon, on the simple stage which she would set, differed, and was of importance, for it concerned Hilda's happiness.

"Maggie," she wrote on a scrap of paper, "throw the Angel into the deepest part of your lake. I adjure and love and trust you my darling Maggie. Yours N. S." Then she tore up the note and wrote "Maggie, keep the Angel safe for me. When I die, throw it into the deepest part of your lake, N. S." She thought, as her fingers folded the note, lifted the lid again and laid the paper in the box, I shan't vex Hilda so much, with the Angel gone.

As she tied and cut the string, she refused to look upon

this act as her deeply significant closing act which, however, it was.

She struck the bell at her side.

"Mrs. Spink," she said, "will you put on your hat and coat and post this box at the main post office. Don't post the letter. Take it, if you please, to the address on the envelope and ask for Mr. Albert Cousins . . . "

"Oh is that the young man who . . . "

" . . . and," continued Mrs. Severance, "ask Mr. Cousins if there is an answer. He will tell you what time he is coming to see me this afternoon. When you come back, will you get out the old whiskey decanter and two of those good glasses, wash them, and fill the decanter, and put them on the little tray . . . "

"Well then . . . !" said Mrs. Spink. "And what are *you* going to do, Mrs. Severing, if you need me like, while I'm away!"

"I won't need you," said Mrs. Severance, in a cloud of smoke. "I shan't try to move, I promise you."

She did not look at the shoe box as Mrs. Spink went with sprightly step out of the room, taking the box and the letter. After all, the box contained her life and she could not look. Her endeared symbol was gone and she would not touch it any more. I have nothing now but the reality, she thought stoically and fairly cheerfully and at this moment it doesn't seem much. I am really too old in living. She recognized for a bright revealing instant that came, and then passed, that life and the evening were closing in. Very well. The fall was a straw in a wind that had shaken her. The Swamp Angel would be safe. So perhaps would Hilda, and happy. The difference, of course, was that the Angel would be unquestionably safe; while Hilda, being only a human being, would never in life be truly safe. This she thought, and more, as, squinting a little, she lighted a fresh cigarette from her stub.

Nineteen

By the time that two months had gone past, Maggie's union with Three Loon Lake was like a happy marriage (were we married last week, or have we always lived together as one?).

The work, divided, fell into its place, and Maggie took easily the essential parts of ordering, providing, planning, cooking – more than that. Sometimes Mrs. Gunnarsen thought that the food was monotonous, but, with that thought, she knew that Maggie suited her meals expertly and without waste to long-distance ordering. She knew that she, Vera Gunnarsen, could not feed twelve to twenty or more people – day in, day out – cheaply and well, and with good humor. Most fishermen stayed only a few days. Many came for the day. Only a few stayed for a week or more, and there was no montony for them. Vera tried, a little grudgingly, to be fair; you could not have it both ways; big menus meant big losses. Henry Corder and the grapevine spread the lodge's reputation, and sometimes some old sleeping bags were brought into use, and still the Gunnarsens had to turn fishermen away. The lake was there, the fish were there, the food was there, but they had not enough cabins and boats. The future reopened before Haldar Gunnarsen. He began to plan expansion in the next spring. Vera his wife, who had hugged hopes of failure and a retreat back to Kamloops, saw unwillingly that Three Loon Lake was in process of re-establishing itself with the help of Maggie. In order to expand still further three things were necessary – youth with physical strength, better transportation, and some capital. If Haldar had been able to find these three things together in Kamloops, he would have done so. But he could not. Maggie gave and left with him a suggestion.

On one of the rare evenings when Haldar, Vera and Maggie had a chance to talk to each other, Maggie told the Gunnarsens about Joey Quong.

"I only saw the boy twice," she said, "and I can only tell you that I liked him at once ... perhaps the circumstances ... I don't know ... but I had such a feeling of confidence that ... " she laughed a little, "I actually spoke to him of some day going into a kind of partnership ... this kind of thing was what I was looking for and I thought he would be good to work with. Of course the boy didn't know what I had in mind and he was taken by surprise. He didn't say yes, and he didn't say no. He's young, active, and nice, and he drives well. I liked his father ... "

"Would you want a Chinese?" asked Vera, whose look had become dark. ("Partnership" – Maggie Lloyd was talking pretty big, wasn't she, Vera thought resentfully.) "And why not?" said Haldar irritably.

"After I got here," continued Maggie, "I heard ... and I'd never heard before ... about the young Chinaman who has that fine fishing place up the North Thompson ... of course, I know, he was born and brought up in the country. But he began the place from scratch – it took lots of imagination and courage – but he did it, and now he and his sister run it and it's a whale of a success. I can't see ... " and she spoke diffidently, because who owned Three Loon Lake? She or the Gunnarsens? " ... I can't see what difference *race* can make ... if you like a person ... and I can't think I'd like any other boy better than I liked that Joey, so quickly. If you want me to, I'll write to him and if he wants to come up, he can, and look at it ... the season's getting on. If you don't, I won't. But you said, didn't you, Haldar, that you couldn't get anyone who wanted to come ... and that you really liked. I'm not pressing it, but I *do* think you'd like Joey. *If* he'd come! They're very dutiful, and even if Joey liked it, he wouldn't come if his father said no ... "

There was a long silence. Dark had come down over the lake. Haldar sat in his big chair, Vera beside him, and Maggie sat on the veranda edge, her legs dangling. There, thought Maggie, I've said my say – if they pass this up, they're passing up a chance, and she could see two pictures. One was a picture of Three Loon Lake lodge, expanding, running smoothly as it well might, with Joey's strength and activity and – perhaps – adaptability, his car, and a stake in the place. The other picture was of the lodge continuing with difficulty and under pressure, until Alan was old enough to supply strength, but no capital, and Alan was a child. Perhaps he would not want to stay with the lodge. No one could say. Oh well, she would be in Kamloops this winter. She already had secured a job there. And perhaps she could find someone for Haldar instead of Joey.

"Write him," said Haldar.

"All right, I will. D'you think," said Maggie, "that it would be a sound idea, *if* he wants to come up, for him to take a run up the North Thompson first and see how things are done in these parts? I don't suppose he's ever given a thought to this kind of thing."

"Okay, Maggie, I leave it to you," said Haldar. Through the night came the familiar sound of a car in the forest. Maggie got to her feet. Lamps burned in all the cabins. Here was someone else who, arriving so late, could not be turned away. Work resumed.

During the weeks there had been a curious reversal in feeling. Maggie had gone on her way serenely. The thought of Edward Vardoe and of the past years seldom disturbed her. The image of Edward Vardoe receded as an image from another life and place – which of course it was. If she had stopped to think – and she had not stopped, she was far too busy – she would have noted that the sharp and cruel visitation that had come to her on the banks of the Similkameen river, then so near in time and space to Edward Vardoe, had not come to her again. It could never come to her again with the same poignance. She had not told the Gunnarsens anything of her life. She had not concealed it, but she had not told it. Vera had wondered. "I wonder why . . . " she had said to her husband. And then "I don't see why . . . " And another time "I think it's pretty funny . . . " and then "When a woman makes a mystery . . . "

Haldar said, "Who makes a mystery?"

"Well," said his wife, daring a little, "this Maggie Lloyd."

"What d'you mean '*this* Maggie Lloyd'?"

"You know what I mean! You'd be the first to say. I just mean it seems pretty funny when a person doesn't tell the people she works for anything about herself. Not that *I* mind."

"Well, for pete's sake," said Haldar, looking at his wife with the harsh difference in his look which she had not seen since the days of their continuous bickering. "'Works *for* us'! For what we pay her I can't see why she works at all except she likes it. I thought you liked her!"

"Oh sure I like her!"

"Well then what the heck." Haldar was angry with his wife in the unpredictable way of a small gale at sea which will, perhaps, die down, or will, perhaps, swell to a storm. He had forgotten his early defenses against Maggie.

"Oh nothing. Can't a person ask a question?"

As this kind of conversation is very dull, Haldar hobbled away and began to trim the lamps outside the kitchen door.

Because Vera Gunnarsen was not intelligent, she could not arm herself against the unexpected and the unwelcome. She could not say to herself At all events, this is better than when . . . or we are lucky now, and once we were unlucky. She had not the support of simple philosophy. When the little sliver of jealousy ran into her flesh, she did not pull it out. Her flesh festered pleasantly round the sliver. She indulged in the pleasure of the pain of her small growing jealousy. Since jealousy is a luxury which soon becomes a necessity to those who have felt its sharp enthralling pain, Vera became unhappy again. She had for some time, now, been that poor Vera Gunnarsen, and habit is strong. There was easy harmony between her husband and Maggie Lloyd. She looked for something more, and there was nothing more. Alan was fonder of Mrs. Lloyd than Vera liked. Maggie had succeeded everywhere where she, Vera, seemed to have failed. Maggie seemed unaware of it. All this was not easy to bear.

Alan, in the kitchen one afternoon, said to Mrs. Lloyd, "Well, go on . . . " His bright eyes watched her.

"Then, of course, he saw that they were Grillians, so he went to the other side of the tree and watched," said Maggie, and took the applesauce cake out of the oven.

"What d'you mean Grillians?" said Alan.

"A large kind of tadpole. I can explain better sometime if we can draw it. Scrape the bowl, I want to wash it."

"You going out on the lake, Mrs. Lloyd?" asked Alan with the mixing spoon half in his mouth.

Maggie did not answer. She straightened up, her face flushed by the heat of the stove and the day, and began counting on her fingers, and over again. Ten quarts of bottled tomatoes stood there, five bottles of tomato chutney, eight loaves of fresh bread, the applesauce cake; two big bean crocks were in the oven. Pies tomorrow. It was all simple fare, and good. Outside in the lean-to, another crate of Kamloops field tomatoes waited to be made into juice and ketchup. "What did you say?" she asked.

"I said Are you going on the lake?" said Alan, taking the bowl to the sink.

"I'd *like* to go," said Maggie. She stooped to put more wood on the stove and damp it down. "We're ready for that party coming before supper and I haven't had a minute to speak to your father and mother. Next thing someone else'll come rolling in and I won't get a chance, and we've a lot to settle before you all go down. So we'll see about the lake."

"Okay. Okay – okay – okay."

"Alan," she said, teasing, and smiling at him, "is that the only word you know?"

"Okay. I mean Yes, okay," he went down to the lake and fiddled about in the boats.

Maggie saw the Gunnarsens coming from their cabin, Vera slightly in front, Haldar hobbling behind. She went to meet them. They stood in the open sunlight, with the tall tree shadows falling toward them. The scent of pine trees, extracted by the sun, was not now observed by the three who stood talking, because familiarity had quenched it for them. Yet it was there.

"Do you think," said Maggie, addressing both husband and wife, "that it would be a good idea if I stayed on for a week or so after you go down by taxi. I'd take things easy. If the weather stayed good I'd take my time, and I might get a bit of fishing. But if the weather broke, I'd hurry and do things up right away and come in the old car before the road turns to gumbo – and bring the perishables."

"Wouldn't be scared alone?" asked Haldar, hesitating.

"Me? No. Why'd I be scared?"

Just about running the place, that's what. Just about running it, thought Vera, standing silent.

"And then," said Maggie, "maybe Vera'd get me a room in town. My job doesn't begin till the first."

"You don't need a room! You'd come in with us," said Haldar blindly.

"No," said Maggie quickly. "I want a room somewhere by myself. She smiled. "You understand that, don't you, Vera?"

Vera remained silent. This was too much. Haldar inviting her to live with them, right there! Without even saying!

"Mr. Gunnarsen, Mr. Gunnarsen!" called a voice from one of the cabins.

"Coming!" called Haldar. He turned and hobbled off.

Vera Gunnarsen looked at Maggie with open hostility.

"What is it, Vera?" asked Maggie. She knew that Vera had changed toward her, and she had divined the causes. If words had to be spoken, let them be spoken now. Haldar had vanished into the cabin with the fisherman.

"You think you pretty well run this place now, don't you. Just about own it," said Vera in a low voice that she could not control.

Maggie looked steadily at her.

The words came tumbling from Vera Gunnarsen, and Maggie listened.

You little damn fool, she thought, you little damn fool. Everything could be perfect. She felt slow anger growing within her.

When Mrs. Gunnarsen stopped talking and was about to turn away, Maggie spoke slowly.

"You little damn fool. You should go down on your knees and be thankful. You *still* have your husband and your child, haven't you?"

Maggie turned and walked down to the dock. The little damn fool, she thought, and she did not know whether she said the words aloud or not.

"Still."

The word hit Vera Gunnarsen. Her passion recoiled on herself. She stepped forward to touch Maggie, but Maggie was on her way down the slope, and her back was uncompromising.

From a window of the lodge Vera Gunnarsen watched Maggie repel Alan who had jumped up at her approach. Alan stood, bewildered. Maggie sat on the edge of the dock, looking down into the water. Alan, kicking the float as he walked, left slowly, and then ran up the slope to the lodge. Vera saw Maggie feel in her pockets and feel in vain, and she saw her wipe her eyes with the back of her hand. What did I say, what have I done, Vera asked herself in panic. Festering flesh does not heal at once; but sometimes it does heal. Jealousy had rejoiced cruelly for an instant at hurting the unhurtable Maggie. And then "You *still* have your husband and your child, haven't you?" How shall I meet her. Oh, how shall I meet her. What have I done to her.

Maggie took a boat and pulled out into the lake. She did not want to go back to the lodge. She rowed out some distance and then let her oars trail. She put her hands into the water which felt cool and pleasant. She bathed her face. Then she rowed on, rounded the dog's leg, and was out of sight of the lodge. She shipped her oars. She was deeply hurt and she was angry, but she knew that she was stronger – and she thought she was wiser, too – than Vera, and that it rested with her to re-establish and maintain relations on which they could all live together. If she could not, her days at Three Loon Lake were over. But, she thought rather bitterly, life is like that – if it's not one thing, it's another; I have not come to a lagoon for my life; one does not stay, ever in a lagoon. Her attachment was strong to Three Loon Lake. Her future was there, and there she could live. Poor Vera. She is accustomed, now, thought Maggie, to being Poor Vera. And she shall, God helping me, be Poor Vera if she wants to. I shall stay out here, she thought, glancing at her watch, for another hour. The food is there. They can manage supper without me tonight. She looked up and, watching a circling osprey, she witnessed a strange sight. She had often wished to see this sight of which she had heard. It now happened.

The osprey cruised above the lake. Maggie, following the osprey with her eyes, was removed from her own thoughts. The big bird suddenly dropped. It hit the lake like a stone. There was a splash, a spray of waters. Then the osprey, free of the water, shook itself like a dog and the spray flew again. The osprey rose, carrying in its claws, pontoon-wise, a silver fish. Now, having risen far above the lake, it turned and with rapid wing motions, flew toward the end of the lake. From invisibility came an eagle. The eagle, with great sweeps and stillnesses of wings, descended upon the osprey. It beat about the osprey with its great wings. The osprey turned, this way, that way. The dark eagle was with him, above him, beating him with great wings. Perhaps the eagle attacked the osprey with his beak. Maggie could not see. She thought not. The battering continued – how long, Maggie could not, afterward, say. The osprey still tried to escape. Then, as if suddenly accepting his defeat, he dropped his fish. Down swooped the eagle. He caught the fish in mid-air and rose. His wings beat slowly and calmly, all crisis over. Maggie looked for the osprey, but the sky was empty. Did a bird's rage or a bird's acceptance possess him? There was nothing he could do. The eagle disappeared into the blue which at the horizon was veil-like, mist-like, carrying the fish, pontoon-wise. Maggie returned to her reality. She had been lifted by this battle of birds with its defeat and its victory. She took the oars and rowed slowly down the lake. Fish rose, and fell, splashing, far and near, and the loon, swimming almost beside her, uttered cries.

As she returned to the shore and reality, Maggie felt like a swimmer who will dive in, and will swim strongly, this way, that way, straight ahead, as he shall choose. But he will swim.

"Where were you?" asked Haldar.

"I felt queer. I went on the lake. I'm all right now."

And to Vera, as she passed, "I felt queer, Vera, so I went on the lake. I'm all right now."

"Where's Alan? Alan, I'm sorry. I felt queer. We'll go on the lake tomorrow."

"Okay, Mrs. Lloyd, okay."

There is a beautiful action. It has an operative grace. It is when one, seeing some uneasy sleeper cold and without a cover, goes away, finds and fetches a blanket, bends down, and covers the sleeper because the sleeper is a living being and is cold. He then returns to his work, forgetting that he has performed this small act of compassion. He will receive neither praise nor thanks. It does not matter who the sleeper may be. That is a beautiful action which is divine and human in posture and intention and self-forgetfulness. Maggie was compassionate and perhaps she would be able to serve Vera Gunnarsen in this way, forgetting that she did so, and expecting neither praise nor thanks . . . or perhaps she would not.

Twenty

E ACH YEAR the idea had been that Alan's father and mother would go up to Three Loon Lake in May before the fishing season opened and that they would take Alan with them. His father might go earlier, because however cold and difficult life might be on that hilltop beside the lake before the ice had gone, Haldar could hardly keep away from his lake, even when it was not possible for him to get much work done alone. There was always work waiting to be done, and while he remained in Kamloops the thought of work waiting there possessed him. There was wood, always wood, to cut; ice to cut and store if possible; repairs to be made; an attempt at new building.

Now that Alan was going to school, controversy arose about taking him out of school and letting him go up with his father, or even taking him out of school later when his father came down and returned with his mother to open up the lodge ready for the fishing at the end of May when business came with a rush. Nothing is more potent and insidious than unanimity about an only child or division about an only child. Alan was used to an accompaniment of this kind of controversy. He was old enough now to be a little useful. Not very useful, but undoubtedly Alan was able to do some little chores that saved his mother's steps, and his father's too, especially now that Haldar (to whom work had formerly been so easy) should be spared steps and movements. One of the things to which Vera awoke none too soon was that this saving of Haldar, which dominated everything, must not be brought home to him by words or even by actions, or he became unwontedly surly and life was uncomfortable for everyone. Haldar's crippled condition and his fluctuating pain had a restrictive effect upon him. This might not have been so if his passion for his property had not been so strong. It was ridiculously strong, and so disproportionate that Haldar began to live in a world of disproportion, where people and events did not exist in and for themselves, but were only adjuncts to his operations at Three Loon Lake and to his inability to perform these operations. Vera had until now been the party in his marriage whose likes and dislikes had been considered or pleasantly ignored, and whose small and frequent complaints had passed unnoticed by her husband, formerly an agreeable man. Thus do our weaknesses betray us. Vera found the whole readjustment difficult to accept and apply. She had an assumption that Haldar's happiness came first with her and that she was the most unselfish of women. It was a good assumption but it was not true. It was easiest for her at the end of a half-done day to say fretfully to Haldar, "Why can't you leave those boats! It's too heavy for you and I'm dog tired working in these cabins. Leave the boats till Rob Rogers comes up. What are we going to do if you strain that hip worse than it is! You look worn out! You're crazy!" She did not seem to know that it was better that Haldar should suffer, and that she should suffer too, if necessary, self-contained and in wisdom. Suffer indeed! They might have been almost happy together if life, not Vera, had been allowed to prove to Haldar that some of his dreams were vain. At first, that was the way Vera spoke to her husband from morning until night, because of her anxiety and imperception, and the old habit of speaking as she felt. At last, necessity restrained her and removed even that small satisfaction. Restraint was forced on her by Haldar who became more silent, then morose, and then turned on her.

"For God's sake, quit nagging or get out of here and go if you can't take it!"

Once Vera said "You love this place better'n you love me. You don't care what happens to me – nor Alan either – if you can just swing this place." Haldar closed his mind to her and with constant physical difficulty went doggedly on. Perhaps what she said was true. Alan, always near, breathed this air.

A child is still one with reality. Nothing intervenes. The light that falls on each day is the first light that ever fell. It has not even a name but it is part of the world of his bright senses. Sounds, objects, air are all his own. They are himself, an extension of himself. And so the grudgingness and disharmony between his father and his mother were accepted into Alan, too, and became an extension of himself. He did not like something in the air. It had no name, but it made him uneasy. He often seemed to be wrong, or to blame, and he began to feel vaguely guilty – of what? Because the stove had gone out; because the stores had not come; because the day was wet. He often slid away, into the woods perhaps, or down to the water's edge where he crouched as by animal nature over the moving water, or over an arrangement of pine cones and a beetle, or over moss into which he poked his fingers, or over a nest of small writhing baby snakes, or he looked up at a chattering chipmunk or up at nothing but a maze of branches and the sky. All these things were part of himself, not very different from himself and he was welcome with them. Sometimes he was cruel, as when he dismembered a fly heavy with summer heat. I'm a bear, he would say, G-r-r-r-r-r, and a squirrel would look at him brightly, with suspicion. Over everything the sun shone, and there was no passing of time, world without end. Then he would hear his mother's voice "A-lan!" Time would return, and he would be drawn back into another place.

Alan slept in a lean-to on a lean-to. His little room, pinned to the side of his parents' room, was like an outsized cupboard. He slept on the kind of thin straw mat-

tress that seems to be comfortable to little boys. He slept a
sleep sometimes peopled with sliding images, strange yet
natural, and sometimes dreamless and deep. He woke,
and became one with a shaft of light that lighted the
unpainted wooden wall, first as a gleam, then as an
expanding brightness. The light showed him the same
cobwebs as yesterday, hanging lightly heavy, gray, floating
a little, left over from last year. Nail marks in the boards
became peculiarly his. Each had its own different being on
the rough plank wall, and was important in its difference,
being part of himself. It was nice to stay in bed with the
gray blankets pulled up to his chin, watching the boards
and the disclosing light. It was nice to get up. He got up.
He did not wash, unless his mother, remembering, told
him. In the summer he bathed, he swam like a frog.
Sometimes, for some reason connected with his father, his
mother, or himself, his hair was brushed. The loose skin of
his clothes was pulled on. He ate. Talk and silence, all
irrelevant, went on above him. He vanished, and then the
call came, "A-lan!"

The year that the lady – Mrs. Lloyd – came, Alan's
father had brought a cat and her kitten and a dog to the
lake and things were better in a way. But the dog who was
elderly seemed to prefer Haldar's companionship and was
really a comfort to Haldar. The dog neither complained
nor criticized and did not seem to find in Haldar's gait or
his difficulties a matter for question or comment. He
loved and admired Haldar and how solacing that is. The
cat, behaving like a dog, sometimes followed Alan into his
places, all her mystery in her eyes, but she was really
indifferent to him. Sometimes she could not be found
because – ranging far and near – she was occupied in her
cat world, of all existences most secret and, no doubt,
delightful. As a companion she was unreliable and so was
her fugitive kitten.

When Mrs. Lloyd came to the lake, she brought with
her a source of fresh happiness which flowed from her and

reached and encompassed the little boy. It reached Haldar and his wife, too, and, insensibly, life was relaxed and easy for a time. Alan had come to feel that his mother had corners on, but Mrs. Lloyd had no corners. She did not say much. Her gray eyes looked at him, at his very self, in kindness; she did not need to reproach anyone; she had a shining softness, even if she did not touch him. I think she likes me! She does like me! Then the cry came "A-lan!"

One day, a few weeks after Maggie had come to the lodge she went up a grassy knoll from which she was able to see to the end of the lake and round, a little, into the dog's leg. If the boats had begun their leisurely return down the lake – the rowers stopping to cast, taking the oars again, tempted by a rise, stopping to cast again – she could tell that it was time to start the dinner. How lovely was the sight, the lake so mild today, the skies bluely benign and clear. She saw that the boats seemed to have turned and she went down the hill. Walking with her light springing tread she made no noise when she reached the level places. Some distance to her right was the trunk of a large fallen pine tree lying at an angle, with the thick end of the tree supported by another fallen log. Along the fallen tree Alan crawled on hands and knees. When he reached the end of the tree he rose and said "I'm a Mexican leopard!" and sprang to the ground. He picked himself up, ran back to the tree, prowled along the trunk, rose, and sprang. "I'm a Mexican leopard!" Maggie watched the Mexican leopard with fond smiling pleasure. The leopard prowled, spoke, and sprang again. In the leopard's mind a joyful kaleidoscope of bright Mexico and dark Africa swirled and blended. Both were the same to him, and no less real in that place than himself. There came a cry "A-lan!" The leopard looked startled, jumped down, and slipped into the forest. Maggie walked on.

"Did you see Alan?" asked Vera with creased brows. "He hasn't done his wood."

"No," said Maggie. She thought That's not fair to Vera but it takes God himself to be fair to two different people at once. What she had seen was a leopard slipping secretly into the forest from which Alan would no doubt emerge.

Twenty-One

MAGGIE MOVED her bed out-of-doors onto the porch which ran the length of the small cabin. There was an overhang of roof. With what delight, when the day was done, she used to lie in her bed looking out at the dark lake, the pale lake, the dark and lighted sky. The excellent air breathed round her in the night. She heard small sounds but they did not alarm her. Lap . . . lap . . . went the lake after a windy afternoon. As she looked at the stars or at the white moon and its shining path, before her eyelids closed, she often heard the cry of the loon, more mysterious in the night. Listen to the melodious wail! Or is it a laugh. Is it a message to the creatures of the lake. Perhaps it announces change of weather. It is indeed mysterious in sound. It clatters and ceases. Owls chuckle melodiously and go silent. Her tormented nights of humiliations between four small walls and in the compass of a double bed were gone, washed away by this air, this freedom, this joy, this singleness and forgetfulness. One night she saw, north of the lake, a pale glow invade the sky. Maggie got up and pulled the blanket round her. The pale glow was greenish, no, a hot color rose up and quickly took possession. The color changed. The vast sky moved as with banners. The sky was an intimation of something still vaster, and spiritual. For two hours Maggie watched enraptured the great folding, playing, flapping of these draperies of light in heaven, transient, unrepeated, sliding up and down the sky. After declaiming lavishly, the great Northern Lights faded with indifference as one who is bored and – deploring display – says I may come back but only if I choose; I do as I wish; I am powerful; I am gone but I am here. The orthodox stars, which had been washed away, returned palely. Night was resumed, and Maggie slept.

A faint light of dawn awoke her too early. Her eyes opened to the gray lake. Passing winds seemed to have left lanes of silver on the water but now the pointed trees beside the cabin had become still. The morning was yet gray and the movements of two phantoms on the rough grass in front of her cabin seemed to be part of sleeping, not of waking. Then she became aware and sat up very slowly. She stayed as still as a stone, filled with instant delight. About ten feet away was a young deer, so young that its pale dapples showed as almost transparent. It seemed more like a concentration of morning mist than a little fawn of flesh and blood. The deer's slender legs were spraddled wide as it gazed down upon the tabby kitten who caracoled, bucked, cavorted and pounced kitten-wise at its feet. The kitten's strong tabby markings showed dark in the pale morning. The kitten ignored the fawn, but the fawn stood, awkward and lovely, intent on the kitten alone. Maggie watched, entranced. The kitten, crouching, feinting, melting silently into kitten curves, darted in small rushes across the uneven piny ground, and the young deer followed, nose down to the kitten, with short deliberate bowing steps. Up and down in the gray morning went the two young things, the watcher and the watched one.

The kitten stopped flirting with herself. Indifferent to the attentive fawn, she moved like an adult serious cat to the cabin, jumped up lightly, and sat yawning beside the bed. The deer stepped delicately to the rustic rail, and, with neck outstretched, kept its limpid eyes on the kitten – large gentle eyes of beauty without meaning. Suddenly the kitten became a family house cat and leaped on the bed, warm with a night's sleep. No longer feral, no longer incandescent, she curled into her comfortable curve and acknowledged Maggie with a pleased green blink. Warm, soft, round, and settled as for hours past and to come, the little cat closed her eyes with voluptuous languor, appeared to sleep, and began to purr. The purr rolled out from the furry little stomach upon the silent and surprised morning. This unnatural noise amazed the fawn which shot forward its large receptive ears, and still gazed upon the kitten. (This is a sight of perfect innocence; it is some enchantment, thought Maggie, and I cannot share it with anyone.) Soon, in the thicket close by, the first bird chirped, and the deer turned quickly at the sound which fell into the air with a tinkle as of glass.

The day was clearer now, and with the real dawn the birds awoke, so that little by little the callings of the birds to the morning filled the spacious air. Still stood the deer.

The kitten awoke, completely aware of birds in the woods. She jumped down and trotted along the veranda and onto the ground. Then, flattening herself, extending herself paw by predatory paw, she passed crouching into the forest. Close behind her stepped the fawn with its delicate bowing tread. The woods received them. Vanished were fawn and tiger.

Maggie did not see this sight again. The Northern Lights did not return. Nevertheless, at night she lay, alive to each sound and sight of the dark; she fell asleep too late and she woke too early. This will not do with all that work ahead, she said to herself, and moved her bed indoors again.

Twenty-Two

A T THE busy time (and after a week or two every day was busy time) Maggie could not always have a swim. But sometimes, in the middle of the day, when the boats were up the lake and the bulk of her cooking was done and the lodge was in order, especially if Vera, who looked after the cabins, or Haldar were free to receive and settle-in any fishing people who might arrive, Maggie had a swim. There was this extra feeling about the swim: Maggie's life had so long seemed stagnant that – now that she had moved forward and found her place with other people again, serving other people again, humoring other people, doing this herself, alone, as a swimmer swims this way or that way, self-directed or directed by circumstance – Maggie thought sometimes It's like swimming; it is very good, it's nice, she thought, this new life, serving other people as I did years ago with Father; but now I am alone and, like a swimmer, I have to make my way on my own power. Swimming is like living, it is done alone. She pushed away the knowledge that Vera was quick in liking, but quick in disliking, quickly resentful, quick to be kind, quick to find fault, sometimes sulky, holding her resentment. What should that matter, thought Maggie, because that is something I cannot help. I will swim past obstacles (Vera is sometimes an obstacle) because I am a strong swimmer.

I think I can go now. . . . "Is it all right, Vera, if I go for a swim? Do you need me? I won't be long."

"No. Go," said Vera cordially. "Do go."

Maggie stands on the dock and looks around her. She is contained by the sparkling surface of the lake and the pinetree shores and the low hills, and is covered by the sky. She dives off the dock, down into the lake. She rises, with bubbles, shakes her head vigorously, and strikes out.

Her avatar tells her that she is one with her brothers the seal and the porpoise who tumble and tumble in the salt waves; and as she splashes and cleaves through the fresh water she is one with them. But her avatar had better warn her that she is not really seal or porpoise – that is just a sortie into the past, made by the miracle of water – and in a few minutes she will be brought to earth, brought again to walk the earth where she lives and must stay. Who would not be a seal or a porpoise. They have a nice life, lived in the cool water with fun and passion, without human relations, Courtesy Week, or a flame thrower.

The water, that element that bears her up and impedes her and cleaves and flies away and falls as only water can, transforms her, because she can swim. If she could not swim, ah . . . then . . . it would no doubt kill her and think nothing of it. But, since she can swim, she swims strongly out into the lake, forgetting past and future, thrusting the pleasant water with arms and legs, and then, quite suddenly, she turns on her back and floats. She is contented. She is not a seal. She is a god floating there with the sun beating down on her face with fatal beneficent warmth, and the air is good. She averts her eyes from the sun and drinks in the upper blue; and then she inclines her floating face toward the shore where the vertical pine trees make a compensation with the horizontal lake on which she lies so gloriously. She could never sink, she thinks (but she could). Maggie was the only moving thing on the lake, making a far-carried sound with her swimming; but now she lies still, and the shores and the water are quiet except for the loon who, down the lake, under the sun, lets loose her vacant musical cry. Turning like a seal, like a god, Maggie swims slowly back to the shore and climbs up the dock ladder. The drops of water rain off her and she feels very fine but she is not a god any more. She is earthbound and is Maggie Lloyd who must get the fire going and put the potatoes in the oven, and she must speak to Mr. and Mrs. Milliken and their two boys from the far cabin who are standing on the dock and are not gods either. They want to know how the water is. Maggie, shaking the wet hair from her face, says it is fine.

The god and the seal are out there in the water. Or perhaps they are not there unless the swimmer is there too. That is a point which philosophers cannot determine. In her cabin Maggie makes haste, and changes.

Twenty-Three

ALBERT COUSINS proved very helpful in the matter of the police and the gun. The police were sensible. They seemed to think the complaint was frivolous. Mrs. Severance thought that Albert had handled the whole thing very neatly.

This was now the fourth visit that Albert Cousins had paid to Mrs. Severance. She sat with her bandaged foot upon a footstool.

"You'd better stay to supper," she said. "I instructed Mrs. Spink how to make a huge dish of spaghetti and cheese and mushrooms and tomatoes and garlic last night and Alberto came but he had no appetite. I hadn't the heart to gorge spaghetti of all things in front of Alberto – the way he looked – so I had an egg, which was nearly as bad. We didn't open the wine, so we'll have the wine if you'll stay tonight, and the spaghetti hotted up."

Albert Cousins said that he would be very glad to stay and have spaghetti and wine with Mrs. Severance, and then he told her about a very strange coincidence that had happened to him that day. He said what did she think about coincidence.

"Coincidence," said Mrs. Severance, "seems to me to be what a Japanese friend of mine used to call 'a series of combination of events' which meet at a certain point of time or perhaps place. It is not as uncommon as people think, and the older I grew the more I believed in the fantastic likelihood – whether relevant or irrelevant – of coincidence, and I still believe in it. I'll tell you a coincidence," she continued (and thought Don't people always), "and then I'll tell you another.

"Once upon a time Philip and I went to New York. I had a friend who lived in New York and her name was Marietta Ward. She lived alone. Her husband had died a few years before and Marietta had never got over it. She never did. Her husband used to call her Peg. There were only two other people who called her Peg and I was one. I hadn't seen her for – oh – years. I found her name in the book, on her street, and rang up, and a voice on the telephone said:

"'Hello.'

"I said very eagerly 'Hello Peg!'

"There was a pause and the voice said in an agitated way 'What did you say? What did you call me?'

"So I said 'Isn't that Mrs. Robert Ward?'

"And the voice said 'Yes.'

"And I said 'Marietta Ward?'

"And the voice said – and still there seemed something strange – I heard her breathing – 'Yes.'

"'Oh,' I said, 'Peg, this is Nell Severance!'

"'I don't know you,' she said.

"Well Albert, I didn't hang up, thank goodness, although I'd begun to feel all queer. I began to say 'Do listen. I have a friend Mrs. Robert Ward . . . ' and then I explained, and she began to cry. 'Oh,' she said, 'I am Mrs. Robert Ward too, and I live alone, and Robert died in January and my name is Marietta and he is the only one who ever called me Peg.'

"Then Mrs. Ward and I looked at the telephone book, each at our end of the line, and there were Mrs. Robert H. and Mrs. Robert L. on the same street, and I hadn't noticed because it was the right street. And they were both widows (the other was my friend, of course), and were named Marietta, and their husbands had called them Peg. There's no meaning in that . . . it's just what happened.

"And I'll tell you another," continued Mrs. Severance
to Albert Cousins. "When Philip and I lived in Burma we
went in from Rangoon to where there were some temples.
A priest said 'There is a man here whom you must see,'
and there was a white man living in that village. So we
went to the villager's house where he lived, and his name
was Philip Severance! He was an American and my Philip
was an Englishman. It didn't prove anything . . . it was
just coincidence and it felt very strange indeed. Of course
when you get into the higher flights, coincidence is sometimes   called   Providence – I   mean   when   coincidence moves to the benefit of some people . . . or some
situation."

"Do you believe in Providence?" asked Albert Cousins.

Mrs. Severance paused. (She thought of Mrs. Spink . . .
I couldn't say, I'm shaw.) "I went to school to one teacher
every day for more than forty years . . . and I still don't
know," she said. "If by 'Providence' you mean (as the
word would imply) a provider who in fact provides cakes
and ale for a thousand people and no bread and milk for a
million people and no rice and whatever-it-is-they-drink
for a million people . . . well, 'Providence' is just a word
and I don't believe in that kind of Providence. But," she
said diffidently, for she had not spoken of these things for
a long time, "it seems to me that one has to move on to
the . . . ultimate . . . that's God . . . it makes things very
complicated but quite simple. . . . Yet there is still coincidence."

"What *do* you believe?" asked Albert Cousins.

She thought for a moment, scrutinizing the end of her
cigarette. "I believe in faith."

"Faith in what?" he asked.

Mrs. Severance did not answer.

"Faith in what?" he asked.

(Really, it might be Philip speaking; only he doesn't
look like Philip.)

Mrs. Severance screwed up her lips, looking downward,

and so made an expression that seemed to Albert Cousins skeptical in the extreme. He waited.

"I shall not tell you today," she said, "I shall tell you another day. There is too much to say about it."

"You are cheating."

"No, I am not cheating. I believe in faith. I believe in God . . . and in man, to some extent. I really shall tell you another day. Now go and let Mrs. Spink know you're staying for supper."

He went, and came back, and sat down again in the chair facing Mrs. Severance.

"When my father first began the business . . . " he said, jerking a little in a way that betrayed the fact that at one time he had been shy. Perhaps he was still shy.

Albert Cousins talked and Mrs. Severance listened, with her eyes on him.

Hilda Severance, coming lightly up the steps, poised and paused for one moment to look in at the window before going into the house. She saw her mother sitting in the accustomed place, listening to a man who sat opposite to her. Hilda could not see who this was because the chair had a solid back which concealed the man who must have been describing or explaining. His hands moved outward in explanation.

Mrs. Severance listened with her habitual look that was both disillusioned and indulgent.

She turned aside her head to blow a spiral of smoke away from him and her eyes looked through the window. Her face changed. Her face shone. She spoke. She took hold of the arms of her chair and tried to raise herself. The man sprang up, and Hilda, turning, putting down her baggage, found the door suddenly opened by Albert Cousins.

Hilda exclaimed. She looked up at him with all the holiday in her face, and this return. And then – What has she been up to now, she thought at once. She looked at her mother and saw the bandaged foot. "Mother, what have you done?" she cried and hurried across the room, sinking down beside her mother's chair.

"It was a trap. I trapped him with it," said Mrs. Severance. "Albert, tell Mrs. Spink three."

"But what *did* you do?" asked Hilda, laying her hand gently on her mother's strapped ankle and looking earnestly at her. "And what *have* you been up to with Albert?" she murmured, as Albert came back from the kitchen.

"I'll tell you about it. I fell," said her mother. "But first. Was it nice?"

"Did you have a good time?" said Albert Cousins in the same breath. Hilda still looked with surprise at him, so strangely at home in her home. He stood there, looking down at her, tall, fair, rather wispy, pleasant, liable at any moment to grow a beard which she would applaud. She had for some time divined in him something which, with her own hesitating permission to herself, she could dare to love, and here he was.

Mrs. Severance was thinking Well, I hope to God they'll show a little sense between them. Albert can take over from here . . . I've had enough. She looked away, and her hand moved automatically to the table. Her fingers sought something and then lay still. Something in the room became simple again as Hilda, scrambling to her feet, began "It was marvellous . . . " and the listeners felt freshly in the room the sea and the road and the wind and the wheeling crying seagulls which she had brought in with her, which were still there, fading, fading away as she spoke.

"Oh it was divine . . . !" exclaimed Hilda. "We went as far as Comox and up to the Forbidden Plateau, and I *must* tell you . . . " Mrs. Spink pushed the door open with her hip.

Twenty-Four

HALDAR CAME into the kitchen.

"We should have got an answer from that boy, the Chinese boy. You wrote him, didn't you?" he said.

Maggie looked up. "Not yet."

More than once Maggie had set about writing to Joey, and then she did not write. A current was flowing through their lives and it flowed from Vera. There was no current, and then it could be felt again. That indwelling *arrière-pensée* which makes one ill at ease made Maggie ill at ease. Each act of hers which was beyond routine caused Vera to manifest ill feeling, not much ill feeling, just a small ill feeling brushed away by a little sudden sweetness. Maggie began to experience some of the self-consciousness which she had formerly felt with Edward Vardoe, but now the tenuous relations between herself and Vera did not stop at Vera but seemed to draw in Haldar and the little boy. Maggie must do well, but not too well. She must be responsible, but not too responsible. Vera was able to create a feeling of guilt in those near to her. Therefore Maggie had not written to Joey, preferring rather that Haldar should think her negligent than that Vera should think her possessive – a situation as light as a cobweb, as strong as prison, and sillier than a poor joke.

"You really *do* want me to write?"

"Of course. I thought we'd settled that weeks ago!"

Maggie wrote to Joey, and close on receipt of her letter, Joey came.

Twenty-Five

NOW MAGGIE stood alone, listening to the last sound of Joey's car, fainter, fainter, really gone. She was alone for further than voice could call, further than loon could cry. If belated fishermen should come she would not turn them away. They could stay overnight and she would feed them with what she had; and they could fish, and then they must go. If the weather held, and food lasted, she would stay here for three weeks, but first she must waste no time before cleaning out and closing up the cabins and the lodge. When that was safely done against the winter, she could let go this tight wire of work, rest her hands, and take her holiday. Her companions would be the chipmunks and the squirrels scampering, stopping, getting ready, too, for winter. The handsome gray whiskey-jacks would grow bolder, too bold. So would the bluejays. Perhaps she would, if she stayed long enough, see the sandhill cranes in their flyways. The sound of the cranes' silver music approaching in all that silence would take her at once out of a cabin with her broom, and into the open, to look up, to listen, and, when they had passed over, to recapture the sight and the silver sound which moved on over other lakes and hills. She would walk up the long overgrown trail to the far end of the lake and, in the evening, approach softly, and stand, waiting to see the heads and backs of beaver in the water, leaving their lodge and returning again. She would hear the gunshot sound of the beaver's tail upon the water as, startled, he dived. She would examine the stumps of the birches, neatly chiseled to clean points by the sharp teeth of the sagacious beaver; then, with her flashlight, she would pick her way home to the lodge, hearing sometimes a stealthy movement in the forest. She would fish.

She went to the cabins and stood at each doorway in turn, estimating what had to be done, and what must be repaired in the spring. She came at last to her own small cabin, and there, on the bed, she saw the parcel – about the size and shape of a shoe box, it was – that Joey had brought with him from the post office in Kamloops. It lay where she had tossed it.

Joey had come in the midmorning. He had driven most of the night. He had breakfasted in Kamloops, had seen Henry Corder according to Maggie's instructions, had gone to the store and the post office, and had driven on, up the hill, past the high lookout over the joining rivers and the town, past the Iron Mask mine, on up into the hills. Young Angus was with him, sitting owlish behind his spectacles, beside his older brother. The boys had driven with few stops from Vancouver to the North Thompson road, up the mountain to the lake where the young Chinese brother and sister – native born like Joey and Angus, but country bred – had their fishing camp, down the road again, up into the hills, and now here they were. Joey slid from behind the wheel and walked with his easy lounging tread to where Maggie stood, her face alight, her hands outstretched. Angus stumped behind his brother.

Joey coming toward her in this so different place drew a veil of sunlight across the rain in Chinatown, the tension and the pitch of emotion in the blackness of the taxi, the crowd in the bus station where were, as if unchangeable, fundamental, her clear memories of the Chinese boy. Mrs. Lloyd, standing in this sunlight, was a different person to Joey from the tired yet strong woman whose side he had taken, somehow, as against some person or persons unknown who were not on her side. Her face was tanned and healthy, and her gray eyes looked surprising in the tan. She wore a shirt and blue jeans and she belonged to this place. Joey did not think these things, but they composed the picture that he saw. A dark man of strong build stood there, leaning on a stick. A woman came from one of the cabins. A little brown boy in swimming trunks ran up from the water. The place looked very nice.

"Joey!" cried Maggie, "and who's this?"

"It's Angus, my kid brother," said Joey.

"And this is Mrs. Gunnarsen, and Mr. Gunnarsen, who own the place. And . . . come here, Alan . . . this is Alan." Angus and Alan were watchful.

Maggie then did some invisible stage managing. She went to the kitchen, while Haldar, walking slowly, showed the camp to the boys. Alan went with them. Vera packed. Maggie prepared a meal.

When they had eaten fried trout and bacon, homemade bread, tomatoes still smelling of the leaves of the tomato plant, apple pie and coffee, they all went out onto the veranda.

"Do you always feed them like that, Mrs. Lloyd?" Joey asked. "That sure was a swell meal!"

"Just about," said Maggie.

"I was thinking . . . " said the boy. "If you had kind of a stand off from the house for parties that came for the day. Give em wieners or somep'n. Like they have in Stanley Park down by Lumberman's Arch . . . save you a lot of work . . . "

Haldar and Maggie hesitated, and then Maggie spoke. "This is different, Joey. A fishing place . . . well, you want to keep it like this . . . " and she spread her hands, pointing. She saw the litter of the hot-dog and fried-potato stand, the paper droppings of the people like the droppings in a poultry yard; and she realized how new to this boy's eyes was the casual untamed scene. The very cabins were as trees in the forest. Joey was pure city. Perhaps it would never do.

As he sat on the veranda, replete and still, Joey was

aware of some enormous difference. This stillness. So it would be like this, would it. His restless eyes ranged the lake, the shores. Joey did not yet know Time that flowed smoothly, as in this place. In all of his life Time had jerked by with a rat-tat-tat, with the beating of a clock, with shrill cries to come to supper, with the starting up of an engine, with the slamming of doors, with the change of radio program, with the traffic, with voices, the fire engine, the change of the traffic lights, separately and all together. He did not think of these things, but it was their absence that made the enormous difference.

Maggie glanced at the boy's face and glanced away. The skin of a smooth yellow beige, was drawn over fine aquiline bones. She thought again, Yes, he is a young priest in a monastery, a young lord, a young Chinese taxi-driver, a young boy sitting on the veranda edge, reflecting, choosing what, thinking what. He was thinking Tennis. I'd never get down to the park for tennis with the kids. Well, I don't get down often now. Less and less. Look, now, at the tennis courts at Stanley Park and the Chinese players – some of them dressed in white – who were his friends, and were not taxi drivers but had day jobs that let them go down and play steady every evening in spring and summer and fall. And now they were far out of his class because he hadn't the kind of time it takes to play tennis and some of those kids were going in for tournaments now. I'd have the winters in town and the summers up here, I guess. No, more than the summers. He reviewed again with critical pride the place up the North Thompson. People coming and going, there'd be lots to do, and spot cash. It's a nice place. A nice life. Haldar Gunnarsen smoked his pipe and said little.

Angus, full, happy, comfortable, with no dreams of tennis, said ingratiatingly "What about me staying to help the lady close up?" Maggie smiled at his round dark peasant face with the thick glasses. If I could just get out on that lake, thought Angus who had never been in a boat. If I could sleep in one of those cute little houses! If I just could!

"No you can't," said Joey, getting to his feet. "We never asked Mother and Dad. You gotta get home for school. We gointa leave right away. If it's okay by you, Mr. Gunnarsen, we better get going."

The boys lifted out some supplies and a parcel from the car. Angus handed the parcel to Maggie and the boys carried the cartons to the kitchen. They piled the Gunnarsens' gear into the car. Oh, thought Maggie, watching, to have a young easy-to-get-on-with man round this place, to haul up the boats, to drive, to pile, to fetch, to lift! The three boys got into the front of the car and the Gunnarsens sat behind, surrounded by gear. There were farewells. Everyone waved. Good-by. Good-by. Take care of yourself. Good-by.

"We'd need a jeep like that guy up the North Thompson on this road, Mrs. Lloyd," called Joey before he drove away. Good-by.

Maggie looked round the empty glade. She was pleasantly elated. "We'd need a jeep." Was that a hope, and, if a hope, was it idle? Vera, Joey's parents, Joey himself, a hundred unknown small interceptions of fate might block the way. She cared, but she would not care too much. When the boys were at home again, their enthusiasm might be lost in the city's familiar din and the intimate publicity of Chinatown. But it's a chance, she thought, and a good chance, or his father with the good face would not have let him come. And what about Angus if Joey doesn't come? She would settle for Angus, gladly. And would Haldar settle? She thought so.

That night, Maggie had a dream which was a nightmare. She stood again in the empty glade. Joey had gone, taking with him Angus and the three Gunnarsens. As before, she stood alone. Out of the wood, as if it had been waiting there, walked a small jaunty figure, doll-like, familiar, neat in its good suit and hat. Edward Vardoe, incongruous in the glade, dreadful for her to behold, walked toward her without sign. She fought an impulse to turn, run, and barricade herself. Yard by yard he neatly came on. She stood still. He came on. Her heart beat to suffocation but she would not move. Edward Vardoe drew nearer and nearer to her, his eyes upon her, expressionless, walking with jaunty steps over the piny ground. She clenched her hands at her sides and stood strongly; as her heart pounded she told herself "I am not afraid. I can smile. Look, I am smiling!" Edward Vardoe was within six feet of her. She saw the familiar brownish suit, the tie, the brown spaniel eyes, the face which changed as she stared from the face of a young anxious boy in a store to the face of a mink that showed sharp teeth and ran screaming into the bushes. She woke and shook herself free of her dream and lighted her candle.

This dream, induced at this moment in some subterranean course, had shown her clearly the face and person of Edward Vardoe. Never, never, from the beginning, she reflected again – and this was strange – had she been able to summon Tom's face. She could call to sight his walk, his manner of sitting, or turning, all characteristic of the man but disembodied, appearing as a walking, a sitting, a turning, a looking. She could not see his face. As she sat up in bed in the cabin at Three Loon Lake she tried again to summon Tom's very face and feature; but for the thousandth time the face of Tom eluded her. And yet he, dead, not to be seen, was her reality; and Edward Vardoe, possessing neither vice nor virtue, a tissue, an interim, was at any moment visible to her and could come, even if she did not call. It's beyond all reason, she said to herself, looking into the shadows of the cabin, but there it is.

She smoked a cigarette, dropping the ashes thoughtfully into her yellow bowl, and she knew that she was not afraid. Seeing him again, even in this fantasy – and awakened now – she was dispassionate, not shaken, and saw as from a distance her servitude as though it had been another's, not hers. He'll go to his reward, if any, she thought ironically, and – good lord! – so shall I! She blew out the candle and settled smoothly to sleep.

But now, as she sat on the side of her bed, the car not an hour gone, the dream yet undreamed and unforgotten, she took up the parcel which Joey had brought from the post office. She read at the top "From N. Severance." Dear old Nell, she thought, what is it. She unwrapped the parcel and saw the Swamp Angel.

She took the revolver and regarded its small elegance of pearl and nickel and shape. She saw in the flowing script the words Swamp Angel. She opened the note and read "Maggie, keep the Angel safe for me. When I die, throw it into the deepest part of your lake. N. S."

Maggie turned and turned again the Swamp Angel in her hands. What has happened, she thought. What has driven her to do this. I shall not see her again. She will not tell me. I shall not ask her and I shall never know. I suppose I'll never go back to the coast ... and she saw (why?) as on a wild day, the shallow sea of English Bay torn up by the roots and flung down again, and the petulant seagulls floating, suspended high up in the wind, and tall trees on the park shore reeling in the sea wind ... and I shall not see old Nell Severance. It doesn't really matter. But what has happened?

Twenty-Six

A LAN SAT between the two Chinese brothers in the front of the car, all very comfortable. All three smiled at nothing in particular because they were enjoying themselves.

Haldar had got into the back of the car with some difficulty. Vera sat beside him, and the boys had piled baggage about them. The car traveled quickly but not too quickly up and down the narrow track, slowing at the curves. Haldar relaxed. He looked at his wife.

Vera's eyes were closed. Haldar had a rare feeling of compunction. "Tired?" he said.

Vera turned her little insignificant face to him, smiled faintly, and said "A bit."

Haldar did what he had not done for many a day. He put his hand over hers with a rough pressure.

Oh, she thought, how good, how good. He seemed as though he had forgotten me. Almost as if he disliked me. She thought Can I speak now while he's gentle like this? She thought Is this my chance to speak?

She thought (but not long enough) and then she said in her folly "I wish I never had to see this place again."

There was a pause. Haldar withdrew his hand and said harshly "You don't have to."

Vera sat immobile. This, then, meant that Haldar had chosen. He had really chosen the lake, and he, crippled, would willingly come back here, alone. She could stay in the town if she wished and he would be indifferent, but he would come back. How hard he was. Now, too, Maggie had restored his confidence as she, Vera, could never have done. How could she let him return, and perhaps with Maggie, and what would people say. Misery welled up in her. Why did I speak. The car proceeded, turning and turning around the bends of the high trail. Only three bends ago, she thought, only four, Haldar laid his hand on mine and he was kind, and I had not spoken, and now I've spoken and I've thrown it all away.

"Forgive me," she murmured, but Haldar did not seem to hear, and she could not tell at all which way his feeling worked – to relent or not to relent – because he was so hard.

Vera, sitting close to her husband, crowded by a little rocking chair, a gunny sack, some cartons, thought It's Maggie Lloyd. It seemed as though her mind reverted continually to Maggie. What is it? What does she wear, do, be that makes her like she is and different from me and better than me and all so quick. She wears a cotton dress, or a shirt and skirt, and so do I, or she wears blue jeans. Vera thought with a little satisfaction She shouldn't wear these jeans; she shouldn't wear slacks; she's too big; she's let her figure go . . . the sight of Maggie, happy, beloved, passed and repassed before her mind. Vera, in her frequent moods of self-pity said to herself I never had a break, did I, my mother never loved me . . . and now . . . look! no, I never had a break. She carried her childhood on her back, and could not – or would not – set it down. Jealousy, how potent it is, the very agent of destruction, a seed that grows. No, a poison that spreads and infests every part. No, the worm that consumes and never consumes. How shall a mind be purged. Vera tried to remember Maggie's look of pain which had reduced her to Vera's place and made them one when Maggie said "You little damn fool, you *still* have your husband and your child!" To give Vera credit, she clung to that moment. Only the memory of the moment which reduced Maggie to past trouble endured and poignantly remembered, when sympathy had rushed from Vera to Maggie, could banish the fiend in her mind. If she could hold that moment, as with her hands, the way might be clear for her and for Haldar, for Alan, and for Three Loon Lake which – she might as well face it – was part of their defeat or part of their unity, and so was Maggie. Her heart told her that. If she, by her venom, succeeded in banishing Maggie that would not be success. She saw herself, frighteningly, and for a moment, as a jealous woman, and for nothing at all. "You little damn fool, you *still* have your husband and your child." It was true; and if she held them too tightly she would lose them. She looked at Alan, little, growing, and hers, in front of her and felt Haldar, silent and miles away, close by her side. I must pull myself out of this, she thought frantically. Poor Maggie. But at the name of Maggie jealousy arose again, faint yet powerful.

"Oh look at Taylor's place! They've got a new barn," she babbled as the fold of a hill into a valley disclosed farm buildings.

"Wonder if Jim built that himself," said Haldar.

"Guess they had a bee or something."

"Jim and Stowe and Blakely built Blakely's barn between them . . . Jim must be doing well . . . he had a good little crop last year. Yes *sir*, that's a nice barn all right," said Haldar, twisting himself to see the disappearing new barn. The blessedness of common things seemed to restore the old common surface between them.

Haldar, who was single-minded and a silent man by nature, pursued his thoughts, half hearing and half responding to Vera. Maggie made a reasonable background in his mind. In every thought and plan for the future there was now included the steadiness of Maggie and, with luck, of one of the two Chinese boys who sat in the front of the car with little Alan between them. As he studied the boys – Joey whom Maggie had first seen and Angus who had appeared unexpectedly today – Haldar thought he preferred Angus. The other fella's got a bit too much personality, he thought; too quick, too many ideas, city ways maybe. Haldar could not figure that Joey would settle down well in this country, not being born here and all. But Angus seemed to want to come, and that pleased Haldar. He was quiet, too, and Haldar liked quiet people. He looked strong.

The road dropped down into Kamloops. Joey drove them to the far end of the town to Henry Corder's house. Henry was a widower and lived alone. They would stay with him for a time, perhaps for the winter. Vera would keep house and had a part-time job in view. Haldar would "look around." Alan would go to school.

The boys unloaded the car, "Good-by, Mr. Gunnarsen," said Joey, "I'll talk to Dad and let you know."

"You do that," said Haldar heartily.

"Good-by," said Angus, and nothing more, no protestations, no promises, except to himself. He hoped Joey would not want to come, for he – Angus – was determined to come back.

Twenty-Seven

"I HEARD that woman Henry Corder sent you was a wonder."

"Yes she was fine."

"Did you like her?"

"I liked her all right."

"What didn't you like about her?"

"Oh I liked her . . . sure, I liked her."

"What's her name?"

"Lloyd. Maggie Lloyd."

"Married or single?"

"Married."

"Where'd she come from?"

"I don't know. She never said."

"'Never *said*!' Got a husband?"

"I don't know."

"You don't *know*? Didn't she tell you?"

"No . . . " abruptly.

"You'd think after a whole summer . . . "

"I know," with a half smile, "but she didn't."

"Does Haldar like her?"

"Oh sure. Haldar and Alan are crazy about her."

"That so."

In the evening Alma Bower said to her mother Mrs. Pratt, "I don't think Vera Gunnarsen's so crazy about that Mrs. Lloyd."

"Lloyd? . . . Lloyd? . . . oh, Lloyd. What's wrong with her?"

"Kind of a myst'ry woman."

"Who said?"

"Well, Vera didn't *say*, but she was sorta cagey. You know Vera . . . Haldar and Alan are crazy about her . . . "

And Mrs. Pratt said to her friend Sally Bate, "Did you hear about that woman's been working for Gunnarsens? Kind of a myst'ry woman Vera says. Vera says . . . "

And Mrs. Bate said to her husband, "You know that woman that's been working for Gunnarsens. . . . You saw her that time you went up to Three Loon and fished. Well they say there's some kind of myst'ry."

"Well she's a humdinger. She looks good to me. She's a nice woman."

"Vera says Haldar and the little boy are crazy about her. Vera's not so crazy herself. I guess she's one of these man's women."

"Well I'll say they *should* be crazy about her, Vera too . . . that spaghetti of hers . . . "

"The way to a man's heart."

"No," said Mr. Bate. "I wouldn't say that at all. I just said it was good spaghetti."

And Mr. Bate said to Henry Corder when he stepped into the shop for a bit of a chat "Say what's this about that Mrs. Lloyd up at Gunnarsen's place? My wife says there's some kind of myst'ry. Seemed a nice kind of woman. Vera don't seem to like her."

Henry Corder was angry and said things about wimmin.

"Well can you beat it the way wimmin talk. Make up a thing out of whole cloth. She swang that place like nobody's business. She's not one of these mod'n wimmin. I got no use for mod'n wimmin," said Henry Corder who had not left the district for forty-five years but liked the movies and knew all about modern women. "She's just not one of these gabby talkers. Myst'ry my foot! You'd think Haldar had the second ur-r-rge on um. Gabby old cats!"

Mr. Bate agreed and said that Jim Taylor's new barn was a very lovely structure.

Maggie dropped in to see Henry Corder, as she often did on her way home from the store where she worked, to show him something.

"How d'you like this?" she said, and let fall a small object into his palm.

He pulled down the spectacles that he wore habitually on his forehead and said "A new one on me. Like a little Coachman but not a Coachman. What is it?"

"I invented it," said Maggie. "I thought it might be a good fly up at the lake and we'll try it out next season. I'll call it the Little Vera. D'you think she'll be pleased?"

"Sure she'll be pleased ... oh say, something I want to say to you. Someone was asking me where you come from and didn't the Gunnarsens even know ... you know the kinda thing ... and I think if you told them a *bit* ... you don't hafta tell *me*," he said hurriedly, and then with a cackle of laughter "I knoo a Juke up here and he was a myst'ry all right all right and the Juke only wore one soot ... sittn up there in the rowboat fishn in a good brown town soot and he cast a mean fly, and I knoo a countess and she had a mustash up the North Thompson but she wasn't no fisherman and I knoo a bank robber and that kinda put me on the spot. This big country's a good place to get away from sassiety and if you go further north I bet you there's lots of interesting tales. Not that ... "

"No no," laughed Maggie, "No, I'm not a duke or a countess with a mustache or a bank robber, but I cooked in my father's fishing lodge in New Brunswick and then ... " Her face grew serious and then it grew sad, and Henry Corder, seeing this, said hastily "Now you don't hafta you don't hafta ... " But Maggie did. She told him about Tom, and Polly, and her father, and the lodge lost and gone, and her working in the store, but she did not tell him about Edward Vardoe because there was no need to do that. That was as if it had not been. She told him that she was happy now, but before that, and for years, she had been so unhappy that she did not wish to think of it, and that was why, she supposed, she had said nothing to Vera or to Haldar about those years. "It was silly of me," said Maggie, surprised, "and very blind. Of course they would want to know.... I never even thought ... I'll take the Little Vera in to them very soon some evening ... and I'll tell them. Let Vera know, will you Henry?"

Henry Corder was deeply moved by the story of Maggie. He admired and loved her because she told the story plainly and without too much emotion. The jewel of Maggie's integrity shone in her speaking, and when, one evening, in Henry's shabby living room, she told the Gunnarsens, with apology for her stupidity in not telling them before, Haldar was deeply moved, and Vera, too, and the story bound Vera to Maggie with Vera's uncertain and wayward love.

For some time to come Vera did not disparage Maggie but praised her and told people how wonderful she was, and uncertainly loved her because it was plain that Maggie had no heart for any other man and only a woman's heart for a child. As yet, anyway, whispered Vera's malignant ghost.

Twenty-Eight

HILDA MOVED for a short time within a luminous cloud, such a cloud as makes hard-headed people soft-headed. She had never before given herself up to love; because she was self-protecting, mistrustful of herself and of others, she had not dared to commit herself to love. It was this fear of committing herself to a boring or a fatal relationship that had nearly delivered her into a solitude which she would have borne well enough, well enough. This she would have preferred to a committing of herself and to a breaking away, a shattering of something, a retreat from the impossible to bear; perhaps she was too cautious for she was not by nature cold. She did not know that her young mother had, without considering, thrown herself into her father's arms at the moment that he opened them to her. But she would know, if she stopped to think, that the love which had bound her mother and her vagabond father was not the common kind. And what is the common kind? Answer that. I am too old, Hilda thought, to be so happy; but how happy I am! Dear dear Albert, how I love his face. I see that he is everything that I could ever love, not perfect, altogether charming for me, unpredictable, yet to be trusted, perfect.

One day Hilda noticed with a curious shock that her mother's right hand strayed involuntarily to the table, felt for something that did not appear to be there and was drawn back again. Her mother went on reading.

"Mother," said Hilda.

"What," said Mrs. Severance, looking up.

"Where is it? I never missed it!"

"Where's what?"

"The Angel!"

"Oh, the Angel ... " said her mother, considering. "I sent the Angel away, I sent it to Maggie."

"Why?" asked Hilda, looking at her mother and seeing that something had happened of which she was not aware.

"Why?" echoed Mrs. Severance.

"Yes. Why did you do it?"

"You didn't like the Angel, did you," said Mrs. Severance after a pause.

It was as if mother and daughter had inadvertently opened the lids of boxes, one after another. Mrs. Severance would not mind doing this but Hilda did not wish to look into the boxes. "No," she said honestly. "I never liked the Swamp Angel," and round her and about her – instead of Albert – were the girls in the schoolyard, all those uniforms ("her mother's a juggler isn't it a scream her mother's a juggler") and always the Swamp Angel; the absences, the felt pity, the second place, her father whom she would have liked to love (amused, impatient, listening to her with one leg of his mind and body out of the door), her mother ("next holidays we'll have a *lovely* time darling you'll see"), and always the Swamp Angel. There was a silence and Hilda smiled a faint one-sided smile. She looked sideways and downward. Should she say it? No, she would not say it after all these years.

"Was it some kind of a symbol?" asked Mrs. Severance speaking blindly but the truth.

Hilda looked up. "I suppose so," she said.

"Of what, darling?" asked the mother gently, thinking There were things I should have known, things I should have seen.

"Oh," said Hilda looking downward again, her hands going out this way that way, "I'm not clever like you, Mother, I couldn't say."

She is not going to tell me, said Mrs. Severance to herself, and I shall not try to make her tell me.

"Well," she said briskly, "it was a symbol to me too and when I had that fall – you weren't here, you didn't see – I nearly lost the Angel to some kind of fellows who would have sold it or used it for crime – passing it on from hand to hand forever at street corners, in bedrooms – and it was so much dearer than I ever knew and when a symbol becomes too dear . . . oh I suspect . . . it can blot out the truth. Think, Hilda . . . no, don't think. What I really mean is I suddenly knew I was old and it wouldn't even need rough boys to take the Swamp Angel away from me so I hid it in bed with me, safe, and then I packed it and sent it to Maggie."

"Why to Maggie? Why not to me?" asked Hilda, chagrined.

"You're too near . . . and there was Something. And perhaps you'd have kept it and all your little boys and their friends would have played bang-bang with it in an empty lot . . . and left it there one evening."

"My little boys . . . " began Hilda.

"And first I wrote to Maggie to throw the Angel away, and then I tore that up and asked her to keep it. But if anything ever happens to me . . . if anything ever happens to me!" she repeated with scorn. "How scared we are, aren't we, of the word 'die,' how mealy-mouthed. I mean when I die . . . " Mrs. Severance spoke with indifference, as: When I die. When I go out in the rain or the sun.

Hilda jumped up. Let us not open the boxes. Shut the lids and put the boxes away.

"I'll make some tea," she said.

"Hilda," called her mother after her, "I don't really miss it at all now. Did you hear what I say? I don't really miss it."

While Hilda and Mrs. Severance opened the box lids and closed them again and Mrs. Severance talked pontifically about symbol, Albert Cousins scowled at a glossy handbook dealing with the fishing industry in Brit-

ish Columbia. He promised himself that he'd give Bates
hell for a job like that. Look at that, he said to himself,
you've got to watch every minute or see what you get.
While he was scowling at the handbook a customer waiting on the other side of the counter tapped with fingers on
the counter tap-tap tap-tap, tap and with his foot tap-tap,
can't wait here all day, who does this guy think he is. The
printing press roared and racketed and Albert Cousins did
not hear it but noticed the tapping. Instead of adjusting
his features nicely to the customer he looked up and continued scowling. He said unpleasantly "What can I do for
you." That is no way to treat a customer whatever he
looks like.

The customer stopped tapping and said "Show me a
kind of a setup for handbills ... it's the Faith Healn
meetns next month out Kingsway. Reverend Mystic Pye.
Somepn like this, see. Better quote me on fifty
thousand ... got any samples?" and he shoved across a
scrawled sheet to Albert Cousins.

Five minutes later Albert had lost an order for fifty
thousand cheap handbills and the customer went out with
the paper in his hand muttering as he went. Silly bugger
that ain't no way to get business.

Albert knew that he had violated a principle by showing
bad temper to a customer who moreover was innocent if
offensive. He was still angry about the handbook which
was a high-class job, not like these handbills. Rather than
let that handbook go out over their name he'd scrap it and
do the whole thing again and swallow the loss. He was
usually good-natured but look at this. The thought came –
and chilled him – that he was as near as makes no
difference to being a married man with a wife and family
to support and he could not act like that, showing temper
and losing business. He regarded the handbook again.
There was Bates. Hi Bates!

Albert did not go about in a luminous cloud although
he loved Hilda sincerely. He reserved love for after hours.
He liked Hilda's looks. She had a dark look and line that

pleased him greatly as an amateur of these things each time he saw her or each time he took her out of his mind and looked at her. Hilda's coolness had melted to a tenderness that surprised him and endeared her. Hilda's mother was not tender. She was matter of fact and that suited him too. He felt increasing affection for her.

"Coming home?" said his father putting on his coat and hat with stained hands.

"Coming home to change," said Albert. Now the day's work was done; the discussion with Bates was over; he had controlled his bad temper; adjustments could be made. As he reached for his hat he released from the back of his mind (where she lived) the image of Hilda whom he would shortly see. Albert was constantly surprised to find himself a successfully engaged man. The feeling was good, irrevocable, and frightening.

"Darling," murmured Hilda before dinner, with her face alight.

"Hello kid," said Albert unsuitably and embraced her. As he embraced her amiably there came to him on a sudden the disturbing pang of love, a sort of celestial corkscrew. Marriage coming on.

As the wedding drew near Mrs. Severance became edgy. She thought the conformities and preparations superfluous and boring. She found herself conversing with Albert's mother – a pretty woman – in a false way, with excessive politeness. She did not enjoy this and was glad that at least she could talk to Hilda without inhibition.

"But you don't expect me to wear a *hat!*" she exclaimed with horror. Her cold gray eyes, habitually half closed, stared widely, and where there had been amused scrutiny was the look of one taking flight.

"But of course," said Hilda crossly. "Now don't pretend, Mother. You're just being difficult. Everyone wears hats at weddings. Except men, of course."

"Brides don't wear hats," objected her mother, "and I never wore a hat in my life. It's terrible."

"You're not a bride, and they do wear hats. I'm going to

wear a hat. Mother! Try to conform. Once in a way. I'll take you to Miss Eager's and she'll have something . . . or she could come here in the evening and fit one. Perhaps."

"A hat," said Mrs. Severance. She was not even smoking. She sat dejected with her little hands on her spread knees, the monumental old woman. She looked up.

"Hilda," she said, "I shall feel a fool. Believe me. Darling . . . Perhaps a bit of lace like for the Pope . . . I've never . . . " she brightened. "Could I stay at home?"

The stormy look that had not visited Hilda's face lately, but which lay in reserve, rose at once. It is extraordinary, Mrs. Severance thought, looking at her, what emotion can do to Hilda's face. Look at this storm, all about a hat. Poor Albert.

"No, no," said the mother hurriedly, "of course not. I didn't mean that. I was pretending." ("You weren't," said Hilda.) "And Miss Eager shall come here and it may kill me. Tonight. Don't delay, Hilda."

How like a monument her mother sat in front of the mirror. Imagine making a hat for a monument.

"Not a hair," said Mrs. Severance gloomily with her hands on her knees.

"Just a *little*," said Miss Eager, bending, with arms extended. "You'll have your hair waved, of course. It should show a *little*."

"Never!" said Mrs. Severance. "Never! I will never have my hair waved. I declare it. Cover it up."

"Mother," said Hilda, "with no hair showing at all you'll look like a . . . a . . . "

"Like a Flemish primitive," said her mother. "There are worse things . . . that will do . . . take it away. I'd like some brandy . . . the big goblet, Hilda."

"Not just a bit of feather?" asked Miss Eager tentatively, half in flight.

"A *feather!* My God woman, I'm civilized!" Mrs. Severance was certainly in a very bad temper.

As she sipped her brandy she said to herself I hate women. . . . I never needed the Swamp Angel so much in my life. . . . I was a melodramatic fool to send it away. Nevertheless, and she looked at her gray face, there are compensations. Death will be, on the whole, a treat. . . . Hilda is getting married and she seems to be happy. . . . Albert is a lamb that I must keep my hands off. My funny Alberto remains for a while. A hat forsooth! I miss Maggie. . . .

She sniffed at the goblet, then she sipped again, and the brandy spread its hot little blessings all through her.

Twenty-Nine

Personal Column

Refined Canadian gent. under 40, well fixed, with car,
desires to meet sincere lady in same age group for shows,
drives etc. Good figure essential. Mat. poss. No triflers
please. Box 841.

After the insertion of the above advertisement Edward
Vardoe began to revive. He entered his dream world.

Thirty

A CAR, containing Edward Vardoe and a blonde, drew up at the door of the apartment building. The two people seemed to be nervous or perhaps they did not know each other very well.

"Well here we are. Won't you come in . . . oh pardon *me*," said Edward Vardoe, opening the door of the car and hopping about to facilitate the lady's descent. How ingratiating he was.

"Sure," said the blonde, easing herself out of the car.

Thirty-One

Y OU'RE A lovely little lady. A real womanly woman,"
said Edward Vardoe thinking also of Ireen.

Thirty-Two

THIS COFFEE'S punk," said Edward Vardoe.
"Make it yourself then," said the blonde, turning sulky.

Thirty-Three

"BUT YOU *got* a hat already! You got *two* hats!" objected Edward Vardoe looking at her sharply.

Thirty-Four

WELL FOR pete's sake what did jever come for then!"
shouted Edward Vardoe, very unpleasant.
The blonde continued to weep.

Thirty-Five

Y OU GO to hell," said Edward Vardoe and banged the door of the flat behind him.

Thirty-Six

H E THOUGHT he would try Ireen once more.
"Hello, is that Ireen?" said Edward Vardoe.

"Iree-een, Iree-een," screamed a voice at the other end of the telephone. Then "I thought she was just laying down but she mighta went out."

"Okay. I'll phone again," said Edward Vardoe and went on down to the office.

Thirty-Seven

M RS. SEVERANCE to Maggie.
"I miss you Maggie I miss you. That was an awful wedding. I wore that hat. I'm glad you never saw it. We all simpered. Alberto wouldn't go and I don't blame him. He says Albert is a drip which is absurd. He said Go and see her marry that drip! No! and then he was vulgar. He likes to think that he is in love with Hilda but that is just a pose that he enjoys. He is not in love and I am liable to be stuck with him for some time but that is all right because he is a good boy and often funny. We have bought a dog. You asked me about the in-laws. The father scowls and I don't wonder. He is a politically minded printer. He comes to see me and I give him my weeklies, a nice entente. I like bitter men myself and I don't think his wife notices that he is. She is – was a pretty woman, shallow, lacking that third dimension that includes perception and awareness of other people. She is obtuse. However, she's Hilda's mother-in-law not mine, and Hilda seems happy to be in a nice conventional family at last and it has not occurred to her yet to be bored by her mother-in-law. Albert is a lamb" (just what kind of a lamb, wondered Maggie seeing a sheep face) "and you would like him. He seems indifferent but is thoughtful and has a sense of humor which he will need. Hilda becomes more conventional every minute. He rules her with a rod of silk. He grew a beard for a wedding present for her and she was delighted. They

should be in Italy by now and they will feel quite at home there with the beard on. It was a great satisfaction to me and I know that Philip would have been glad that we could give them that present of Italy from us. They are likely to have two children and no more and Hilda will spoil them with overattention as a compensation for her childhood (yes, I know, my fault). She will consider them perfect. I see it all. She thinks she does not like children but you watch.

"Isn't it strange Maggie – nearly all stories have been about love or fighting and all love stories have been about faithless, unhappy, or frustrated love. No one can write about perfect love because it cannot be committed to words even by those who know about it. I think Albert and Hilda have a very fair working chance. They will not have perfect love but I foresee a nice kind of happiness and am thankful.

"Maggie I miss you very much to talk to and I need humanizing. I'm a bad influence on myself. I used to think my judgment sound and now I mistrust myself. Is there any way I could get up to that place of yours this spring. I could help you with the cooking, you know how good I am. How could I get up. I could stay a week or a month according. Is there plumbing. I regret very much that I sent you the Swamp Angel. I have tried to substitute inkwells and can openers and so forth but the balance in the hand is not the same and I cannot juggle them. The thing was that I saw at that time the finger of Death approaching and I grew sententious. Now I have recovered and while still an unusually religious woman have become worldly again and miss my vain toys. Next time Death whispers in my ear I will take it easy and not get so serious about it and the same for you. I forget, did I ask you if there is any plumbing at the place or just those holes outside. That's fine in youth but for old age it's no good."

Maggie to Mrs. Severance.

"My dearest Nell, thank you for your letter. You didn't

say much about the wedding did you. You're a bad
reporter – what Hilda wore, the bridesmaids if any, the
presents, a reception? their new house, the speeches? You
thought about nothing but your own hat. I fancy you have
behaved very badly over that. About coming up. Let me
assure you at once that I'd love to see you but that I am
too busy to see anyone now that we're going up to get
things in order and when the season gets into its stride, so
I needn't deceive you. I should not allow you into the
kitchen with all your wines and garlic. I cook cheap on
different terms up there – do you realize that we are
twenty-five miles from anywhere? A thoroughly nice
young Chinese boy whose name is Angus is coming up
next week to start in working with and for us, a sort of
partner, because his father is giving him a large old good
car which will be a lifesaver for transportation and if
things go well we're going to get a jeep. Angus is sweet and
strong and biddable and he seems to have fallen for the
place. We've had some very earnest letters from him and
if you really want to come on those bare terms he would
take good care of you. He says 'My Dad operates taxis so
I can assure you I am a rasponsable driver.' Traveling the
way you'd like to travel it would take two days because
you'd stop overnight somewhere. It can be done in one
day's hard driving from Vancouver. There is no plumbing,
just privies, but next year we hope to have it. Nell, I long
to see you, but I cannot fancy you enjoying it up there.
There's nothing but fishing and scenery.

"About the Angel. It may not be very significant to you,
sending it away, but it is to me. It was right to do that.
That mood will return, dear Nell, and you will be glad
that the Angel's safe. I am so sure that our ability to throw
away the substance, to lose all yet keep the essence, is very
important.

"If you decide not to come up, and I dare not urge you,
let us plan to join each other for a week when this season
is finished at some such comfortable place as Kelowna or
Kamloops where you will have all the plumbing you

require and a better bed. Wouldn't that be gorgeous. I will never go back to Vancouver in any case, not even to see you. You asked me in your last but one about my people here. Quite perfect except for one recurring bad obstacle, I'll tell you when I see you. In the meantime I pretend I'm a swimmer and I just swim round it and hope I can continue to do so because this is the place in all the world that I like. I miss you too dear Nell. For me there is no one like you."

Scenery and fishing. "Fishing," muttered Mrs. Severance, reading, scornful, thwarted. "Fishing! Sadists! Bull fighters! People must be mad."

Thirty-Eight

I'LL NOT stand for it!" said Edward Vardoe.
"You bet your sweet life you will," said Ireen.
"But . . . "
"You heard me," said Ireen fixing him with a light green look.
"Okay Ireen that's okay by me," said Edward humbly, hurriedly.

Thirty-Nine

Q UIT LOOKING at me like that."

"I wasn't looking at you like that, honey," said Edward Vardoe.

"Honey yourself and see how you like it," said Ireen. Eyes like a spaniel. Eyes like a dog. Make me sick. "Quit looking at me like that!"

"Okay Ireen."

Eyes of a dog, and a dog's wages.

Forty

THAT WINTER in Kamloops had been very pleasant. Something like harmony seemed to be restored between husband and wife. Alan, getting on for nine, began to be a boy among boys, and rough. This harmony – temporary or permanent – increased after Maggie had told her history, and after she gave to Vera the Little Vera which was highly esteemed. Maggie did not often visit Henry Corder's house. She thought it better so, and she worked each evening in her room at her old occupation of tying flies. She sent most of them to Mr. Spencer in Vancouver and had a constant market. She made some acquaintances. Working at the flies she thought, dreaming, of Polly, so innocent. She could think more easily, more often, of Polly now. It was because of Alan, perhaps – and time, of course.

On Christmas Day Maggie joined the Gunnarsens and Henry Corder. She brought with her a present for Haldar and Vera together, and books and balls for Alan, and some flies for Henry Corder. She had looked for and found in Kamloops a nice long piece of pine wood of good graining about two inches thick. This she had planed down and whittled to a blunt arrow point. Then she had drawn, gouged and carved the words THREE LOON LAKE 7 MILES. This was destined for a crossroad where there was now a bit of wood, faintly marked and askew. She had then shellacked the board and very fine it looked, just like the signs her father used to make at the lodge at Naguisheep. She had never done this before but she had watched her father doing it. Maggie was proud of this piece of work, and indeed it looked very nice and would give style – and confidence, too – to the approach. We need another one to encourage people on the fifteen-mile stretch, she thought, and one as you turn off the road to Lac le Jeune, and then, perhaps the word LODGE or OFFICE. She gave Alan the small set of tools which she had bought, and some more bits of wood to practice on; but it was Haldar who, sitting in comfort, took over the sign making with almost absurd delight. He became much better at carving wooden signs than Maggie. He then carved other signs and sold them to other people in the district.

Then a pleasant thing happened which turned out to be unfortunate. This arose from an incident which had occurred some months before.

There had been a short and bad break in the weather at the lake. The lake had become slate-colored and threatening; rain poured down; then strong wind arose and made casting impossible; those four days were almost time and money wasted for fishermen who either pulled out and left, or stayed for one more day hoping for fine weather again, or went on the lake regardless; but fishing was not good.

In one of the cabins at this time was a man by the name of R. B. Cunningham. Mr. Cunningham was an American and might be said to come from Santa Barbara. Or he might be said to come from Texas where he was raised, or from Mexico where he had interests, or from the Porcupine, or from New York where he certainly had interests, or from northern Quebec; interests took him to Europe also. He was a small thin beige man, with a beige face and beige clothes. His cigars were pale in color. He spoke little, and communications around the stove in the evening appeared to flow above and around him but did not. Each fisherman waited impatiently for another fisherman to finish his tale (whose termination seemed slow but was inevitable) in order to begin a tale of his own. These tales gave inordinate pleasure to the tellers. Tales often collided in mid-air. What annual joy each story celebrated for its owner. His story welled up and burst "That reminds me up at Canim one time ... " These sessions did not bore Mr. Cunningham. He enjoyed them, smoking his cigars and saying nothing. It might not be noticed at what moment Mr. Cunningham's chair became empty. No one saw him go. He was a very unnoticeable man. In his dealings with the lodge people he was pleasant and almost grateful to Haldar, Vera, or Maggie for any inquiry as to his comfort or for any assistance that they might offer; he made few demands and did not need much assistance. The minute his boat was ready he got in nimbly, moved away competently, and could soon be seen in the middle distance, contemplative, casting a fly. Anyone asking Haldar how old Mr. Cunningham was would be told "Old ... well ... hard to say ... might be all of sixty ... maybe more ... hard to tell." Mr. Cunningham was seventy-five. Great would have been the surprise at the lodge if it had been disclosed that at the name of Mr. Cunningham many people in various parts of the world became apprehensive. It was probable that Mr. Cunningham who had a nice fishing lodge of his own in Oregon and one in the Adiron-dacks found the utmost pleasure and restoration in going, in his beige fashion, up to British Columbia – to Tweedsmuir Park, to Fort St. James, to Three Loon Lake, unknown, unsung. Anyway that was what he did when he could. He stayed on, day after day in the bad weather, hoping for a break and actually going out on the lake. Skies continued gray and promised no relief, although at the end of four days the lake and sky suddenly blossomed without warning into innocent beauty and shone with calm, deceitful as a witch.

Haldar noted and commented to Vera upon the fear-lessness of Mr. Cunningham whom he called that old fella. One afternoon Mr. Cunningham, indifferent to opposi-tion from man, market, or weather, set out up the lake.

Fishing might be good because the wind had dropped, the rain held off and – according to his private system – the time was right. So, out he went, the only one on the lake.

There is a *mystique* in fishing which only the fly-fisherman (a dedicated sort of person, or besotted) knows anything about. All fly-fishermen are bound closely together by the strong desire to be apart, solitary upon the lake, the stream. A fisherman has not proceeded far up the lake, not out of sight of the lodge, before he becomes one with the aqueous world of the lake, of a sky remarkable for change, of wind which (deriving from the changeful sky) rises or falls, disturbing the water, dictating the direction of his cast, and doing something favorable or unfavorable to the fish. He is sometimes aware of the extraordinary beauty, majesty, of the clouds, white or angry, which roll up in that weather breeder, that sky not far above, which caps the lake and him. Rain rushes down upon him, but something within him murmurs It will soon be over, and sometimes it is soon over. His eyes, occupied with this business of casting advantageously and making contact with a streak of living protesting silver in the water, are sometimes raised to the shore; and there he sees, in the early springtime, a group of aspen trees standing slender, white-bodied, like dancing girls, poised as if to move away, and beginning to be dressed about their slender arms and shoulders in a timid unearthly green. They are virginal. On the lower slopes from which he has come, the aspen leaves are already out and have assumed a mere green and their lifelong occupation of trembling. But here, on the upper heights, these infinitesimal leaves are yet too small to shiver. They dress the white aspen trees, and the fisherman's eyes, passing rapidly along the slopes above the shore, see also large masses of this ethereal green where an aspen grove stands against the dark coarse magnificence of lodgepole green or spruce. It is a matter of light falling, how green or not green the forests can be. He does not look too long (for he is fishing) but the green and the greens, the blue, the somber, the white, the deceptive glamour of the lake surface enter into this *mystique* of fishing and enhance it, and they enter into him too, because he is part of it. There is no past, no future, only the now. Mr. Cunningham has neither wife, mistress, child, rival, profit nor loss. He is casting into his favorite place by the reeds where he picked up three beauties on Wednesday (was it Wednesday?). He did very well, and experienced this inner rapture which should have been past, forgotten, as irretrievable one would say at the age of seventy-five as intense sexual joy. But no. It is unique and was his. Other fishermen had lurched down to the float and re-examined the sky and had said it didn't look so good and they weren't going to get another wetting like this morning and how about a game of bridge, and not for me, I'm going to have a nap, good day for a nap, might join you later.

The wind got up. It is peculiar to fishing lakes that if a wind "gets up" it gets up with the utmost malignity in the middle or late afternoon when all the fishermen are at the far end of the lake and have to make their way home to the lodge for supper against the wind. It is notorious. They *must* start, and only the fool or the hero will delay and have a few more casts. What a passion it is. Well, up gets the wind, and the fools and heroes have to pull against it and the waves bucket and rock and the oar flies out of a sudden trough and nearly upsets the rower who, looking at the shore, sees that he is not making any headway. That is what Mr. Cunningham did. He pulled and pulled on his oars and seemed to get nowhere. The waves on this small murderous lake, unpeopled as a desert, were irrationally high and fierce, and down came rain like arrows. The wind was implacable. At the head of the lake he had been a wiry elderly man of about – one would say – sixty. He became his age about halfway down the lake and then, laboring, pulling, making little progress against the storm, he more rapidly became an aged and exhausted man, breathing with difficulty, pulling with difficulty, wet through, game, and nearly done. It is a terrible thing to be alone, weak, and in a storm, far from the indifferent shore.

It was not until dinner was nearly over that Maggie noticed the absence of this unnoticeable man. People had finished their eating, finished their table talking, and had pulled away from the little tables; some had gone to the cabins to make an evening of it; three or four were gathered round the airtight heater in the dining room; chairs were scraped along the floor; stories were on.

Maggie did not like to hurry or chivvy the customers about mealtimes but, hesitating a little, she thought she had better go along to Mr. Cunningham's cabin, and knock. She pulled on one of the slickers and went through the driving rain to the cabin. She knocked. There was no answer. She ventured to look in. No one was there and the cabin felt chilly, the air was raw. Maggie went out of the cabin and hurried to the float. The rain streamed off her slicker. Peering, she saw through the grayness of driving rain, curling waves, and failing light a boat approaching very slowly. The oars dipped uncertainly.

Maggie ran back to Mr. Cunningham's cabin and put on a fire in the heater. That took only a minute. The little stove made a hot blaze almost at once. She turned back the bed, and, moving quickly, took Mr. Cunningham's pajamas and placed them on a chair near the fire. She shut the door and ran back to the float. The rower of the boat did not seem able to come alongside. Maggie untied a wet boat, got in, pulled a few strong strokes and reached Mr. Cunningham. She secured the rope at the stern and towed the boat in. Mr. Cunningham sat bowed as in a heap. She tied the boats. She helped and pulled Mr. Cunningham out of the bobbing boat. But he, vaguely motioning with a feeble hand, would not move a step. Maggie, divining, stood him up alone, like a doll, and then quickly knelt and reached down. She took out his precious rod and stained old knapsack. Then, carrying these, she turned to Mr. Cunningham, and, without speaking, but willingly, he allowed himself to be led to his cabin. Down lashed the rain. He was as wet as a sponge.

Maggie opened the cabin door and the warm air flowed out. She turned down the draft of the stove, and lighted the lamp.

"*There*," she said, depositing Mr. Cunningham squelching in a chair, "do you think you can get your things off and get to bed or shall I help you?"

"I think ... my boots ... " said the sodden one, and Maggie went down on her knees.

Mr. Cunningham had not seen Maggie except as a presence, full of help and strength. Who was she. Was she the cook. I don't care who she is. I'm here.

"Have you any whiskey?" said Maggie.

Mr. Cunningham pointed to his bag.

"I'll go and get some boiling water and make you a toddy. Do you like lemon ... sugar?" He nodded.

"You get undressed and to bed and I'll be back," and Maggie went out.

Mr. Cunningham undressed and feebly rubbed his little body with a towel. He stood beside the lovely stove. Then he slowly pulled on his pajamas and clambered into bed. As independent as a mountain, he was not used to being an object of help and compassion, especially to an unknown woman who did not know that he was *the* Mr. Cunningham and regarded him only as someone in need. There was a pleasing novelty but also some humiliation that he, R. B. Cunningham, should have been all but conquered, obliterated, by wind, rain and waves on a small lake. Maggie reappeared with a tray from which steam arose. Before approaching the bed she peeled off her dripping slicker.

"You're wet," said Mr. Cunningham. It was obvious. She was wet. "My things ... " he said apologetically, looking at the heap of soaked garments on the floor. He was a neat man by nature. (The rain beat outside.)

"That's nothing," said Maggie, sweeping them into a

pile. "I'll hang these on the kitchen racks in the ceiling and they'll be bone-dry by morning."

Mr. Cunningham, inhaling the steam of the toddy, looked at Maggie's face.

"Your hair . . . " he said.

"And that's nothing, too," she said, "it'll dry kinky. Are you feeling a bit warmer?"

"Very good," said Mr. Cunningham, not looking very good. "Very good."

"I'll bring you some hot soup and some bread, and you just take it if you feel like it," said Maggie, putting on the wet slicker and bundling up the clothes.

" . . . did I thank you . . . ?" asked Mr. Cunningham uncertainly.

"I don't really know," said Maggie with her special smile, with her rat's tails, "yes, I'm sure you did."

"No I didn't. What is you name?"

"Maggie Lloyd . . . Mrs. Lloyd."

"I'm sure, Mrs. Lloyd," began the small man in the bed, but Maggie, saying "I'll be back," was out of the door. She brought the broth on a tea tray, covered by a towel and covered again by a rubber coat. "It's an awful-looking bowl," she said deprecatingly, "but the soup is good."

Mr. Cunningham looked at the thick chipped bowl and at a chipped jug that contained the soup, and he thought of the margin between what might have been and the validity and comfort of the warmth and of this woman who offered him life in a chipped bowl, with apology. "Try it," she said, looking down at him.

Warmth spread through Mr. Cunningham and a resurgence of spirit. He knew that he had been near the point where Being touches Non-being, and that if the wharf had been fifty yards further off, he would have no doubt have died unless, of course, this Mrs. Lloyd had not come for him. That is, he would have ceased to exist at Three Loon Lake or New York or Santa Barbara, and he would not now be leaning back in bed sipping hot toddy and soup brought to him by that fine woman with wet hair. All his life and lives would have gone. This was not the first nor the fiftieth time that he had pitted himself against the powers of Nature, and he was inclined to take survival as a matter of course and would continue to do so until in the operation of time and chance he reached extinction. He was a survivor by profession. Even now he might have a chill or pneumonia, but his native toughness assured him – and he agreed with it – that he would not have pneumonia. Life seemed to kindle again in him. The cabin, warm to the point of fug, the toddy, a bowl of soup with bread – these simple things spread comfort through his thin body and relaxed spirit. When Vera, stepping lightly, came in later for the tray and to have a look at the fire and at Mr. Cunningham, she saw that he was asleep. The jaw of that powerful and influential being had dropped; he snored lightly; the man in the bed who caused others to tremble looked very small, and old, but unquestionably he was still alive.

When, after resting for a day or two, Mr. Cunningham – wearing his good beige town suit – left on the week-end taxi, he was grateful to Mr. Gunnarsen and to Mrs. Gunnarsen but particularly to Mrs. Lloyd. He did not say You are beautiful, Mrs. Lloyd, with your hair – which is now drying – waving naturally, and your gray eyes so impartial and kind, and your smile so white and pleasing to me, and your bountiful figure and I only a husk of a man now dammit, and you are good.

He only said seriously "You were very very kind, Mrs. Lloyd. I'm sure I'm much obliged."

This incident would have been forgotten or, rather, it would have lain in memory to be taken out the next time that anyone might arrive back at the lodge too wet and too weary if it had not been that, in the following February or March perhaps, Haldar received a letter from Mr. Cunningham. The paper was expensive but not showy; the letterhead was chastely engraved; there was no exhaustive or imposing list of Mr. Cunningham's interests; this was personal writing paper and it breathed a refined opulence

which had not been suspected in the man in the beige suit.
Mr. Cunningham in his letter said that he was diffident
about approaching Mrs. Lloyd about the subject he had in
mind and, as he did not wish to disturb the happy condition of things at Three Loon Lake, he thought it better to
approach Mr. Gunnarsen first. This preamble made Haldar wonder. Mr. Cunningham then offered Mrs. Lloyd the
permanent position of looking after his lodge in the
Adirondacks at a salary that nearly caused Haldar to faint.
He left it with Mr. Gunnarsen, however, to acquaint Mrs.
Lloyd with this offer, or not, as, he said again, he did not
wish to disturb the status quo (what's that, said Haldar,
but he got the sense of it). After this horrific suggestion,
Mr. Cunningham said that he was sending Mrs. Lloyd a
small present as a token of gratitude for her kindness to
him, and he hoped that this present would also be useful
at Three Loon Lake of which he had such pleasant memories. By the way, the offer was always open. He then
remained, Faithfully, Haldar's.

In Haldar's small intensive world which had recently
become a sunny plateau of temperate climate this letter,
though exciting, was as acceptable as a rattlesnake. He
showed it to Vera in dismay, and his baser self told him to
say nothing of it to Maggie, but this, he knew, was
unthinkable. He would have to tell her. Vera, impelled by
different feelings, could not tell Maggie fast enough. She
resented, a little, that Maggie, if she took Mr. Cunningham's offer, would receive an unreasonably large salary
and much glory, but, on the other hand, Maggie would be
removed painlessly, and still the lodge would begin its new
season in a fair position, especially with this Chinese boy
who seemed to be good. Vera did not at once realize that,
with Maggie away, the boy might cease to be good. After
this brief joy, reason reasserted itself and Vera was aware
that without Maggie the lodge would drop down again, the
boy might not stay, and her troubles would be upon her
once more. She hated Maggie for being indispensable,
inevitable.

Haldar showed Mr. Cunningham's letter to Maggie with trepidation. He watched her face as she read it.

Color flowed over Maggie's face and stained her neck; pleasure sparkled from her eyes as she looked up at Haldar. She handed the letter back.

"How lovely! How lovely!" she exclaimed warmly.

Haldar waited anxiously, then "You'll go?" he asked.

"Go!" said Maggie with surprise. "Of course I won't go – not unless you want me to – but how *lovely* to be asked!"

Vera, who could not have things both ways, was then irritated with Maggie for behaving thus magnanimously but found a solvent in the thought that the offer was always open. At present, however, Maggie would remain, the irritant under her skin.

In the meantime Mr. Cunningham had written to a Mrs. Roger Harrison whose husband was his Vancouver agent. He paid his compliments to Mrs. Harrison and asked her to pick out some English earthenware and send it to a Mrs. Lloyd care of the following address. He said briskly that he did not want any of your bone china which was not suitable for a fishing lodge; he wanted a good gay earthenware of cottage type, six dozen of everything, breakfast, dinner, tea. He trusted Mrs. Harrison's taste. Mrs. Harrison was delighted to go shopping at Mr. Cunningham's expense and at once sent up two dozen of everything – a charming pattern – the rest to follow.

Maggie was enchanted. Such a nice thing, such a generous thing, had not happened to her since she could remember. These earthenware bowls and cups and plates which she fondled were honest and gay, and had been conceived by people who were honest and serious and gay, living in the midlands of England, perfecting this creamy base and strong pattern and generous shape to give pleasure to Maggie Lloyd who had built a fire for Mr. Cunningham on a wet night which had not been forgotten by him. These speculative affinities of time and place gave Maggie, habitually, a private pleasure, and the English earthenware assumed a living entity which even its destruction would not destroy, and which was really beloved by her. The present was undeserved – she would have done what she did (so little!) for anyone. But here was something that was hers and would enhance the lodge. "We'll make a Welsh dresser," she said with delight.

Mr. Cunningham's gift seemed disproportionate to Vera who said primly to Maggie "Oh, we mustn't use *your* china! What *we* have is good enough for *us*. Oh, we couldn't do *that!*" Vera, it seemed, could destroy the earthenware.

Idiot, thought Maggie, her pleasure checked. Aggravating idiot.

She turned toward Vera and searched her face. "Vera," she said, "six dozen! It's obviously for the lodge, not for me."

"Well, why couldn't he say so," said Vera, and put more fuel on her private fire.

Maggie's face clouded. She wrote to Mr. Cunningham and felt that she could not sufficiently express her thanks to him.

Many futile discussions now ensued as to Who should go with Who in the two cars to the lake to begin preparations for opening the season. Only Maggie could drive the old car. Haldar would go with Maggie – Vera took exception. Alan would go with Maggie – no, for some reason or other. Vera would go with Maggie – it became impossible somehow. Maggie would go alone, or before, or following. Vera spread dissension in her own heart and irritated everybody. Angus arrived, beaming ingenuous pleasure, happily unaware of conflicts. There were times when Maggie said wearily to herself To hell with the lot of them, and turned her mind to Mr. Cunningham's offer. It was not so easy sometimes to say "I am a swimmer and I swim round obstacles." The words became smug and flatulent. These people were now her family. She had no other. One can say, also, "To hell with the family," but the family remains, strong, dear, enraging, precious, maddening, indestructible . . . and think of Alan. I cannot do without Alan. If I cannot cope with Vera and her folly, thought Maggie, I've failed. She challenged herself, and went on. Haldar, who had felt in some way things were going wrong, knew himself mistaken. He saw Maggie, busy, serene, and knew that things were right. He hobbled about briskly, whistling.

The two cars left for the lake, and Maggie returned with Angus to pick up further supplies. The Chinese boy's unawareness, his willingness, his youthful ingenuousness were consoling.

Forty-One

THE THREE-TIME-A-DAY ever present English earthenware was only the outward cause of Vera's fatal and persistent folly. Her jealousy devoured her – the worm that never dies, the worm consuming her, she was daily and nightly consumed. She sought aggravation.

"Alan," called Maggie from the kitchen, "go to the roothouse and fill this basket with potatoes and then find Angus and ask him to come here and have a look at the window it's jammed or something and then come back and clear your things from the table, I need it. No . . . hurry . . . there's a good boy . . . I want those potatoes now," and Alan loped away obediently.

"You're getting insufferable," said a low voice behind her. Vera had come in with her madness on her. "You're getting insufferable, giving your orders round here. Every day I hear you ordering my husband and my son about and I've kept silent. Ever since you got that china it's gone to your head. You think you own the place. You've got beyond yourself."

"Well . . . " said Maggie, turning to confront Vera whose face was dark and flushed with passion.

Maggie waited a moment and then she said coldly, "You are ridiculous and I will not argue with you. You make life impossible for your cook and if you can't control yourself you'll make life impossible for your husband and your child . . . and you will for Angus." She leaned with seeming nonchalance on the dresser. "I will cook this dinner and then I shall go and pack up my things" (that won't take long, she thought, and she saw the little yellow bowl). "Tomorrow Angus shall drive me to town, right in the middle of the season and you will do the best you can," she said cruelly. "I shall not tell Haldar till tomorrow morning. . . . Now" (and Maggie's coldness broke into fury) "get out of my kitchen, I'm busy, and if you don't shut the door, I will. Get out."

"You'd *dare!*" exclaimed Vera.

"Yes, I'd dare. Get out," said Maggie, advancing upon her, and Vera went, with sudden dismay.

Maggie closed the door and sat down at the kitchen table with her face in her hands. She heard, vaguely, Alan dumping the basket on the back steps and running away. Oh, she thought despairingly, after all this, I've failed. And now it will go to pieces and they will fall apart again. And Angus will be disillusioned by me and by the bickering that will follow, and he will go back home with his first little career over, or he will go from job to job in the upper country. Light fell on the faces of Joey and of his father who had trusted her on one short encounter. Her thought went first to others, not to herself. Her thought dwelt on Vera and the irretrievable muddle and misery that Vera and her jealousy – for it was jealousy – created. She thought of Haldar and Alan and of all that Three Loon Lake might have been to them. And then she thought of herself. For her own future, she was not afraid although she looked forward cheerlessly. It would, of course, be truly said that Mrs. Lloyd left the Gunnarsens in mid season for a rich job in the East, and she would not defend herself. It was of the past that she thought. With all her fine thinking she had not been able to cope with one unhappy human being. Human relations. Human relations. I wish that Nell Severance were here with her acid good sense. Oh to be with old Nell where no one has to act or pretend or swim around. Human relations . . . how they defeat us. Yes, I am defeated. She did not know how long she sat with her head in her hands.

She heard Angus coming onto the porch and Alan's running steps. She smoothed her face with her hands as if to obliterate something.

"Angus, this window . . . look," she said.

Forty-Two

THEN ... *YOU* ... did it," said Haldar slowly.
"I did not!" stammered Vera. "I hardly said a word
and – and she told me to get out of my own kitchen! You
should have heard her! Really now Haldar ... " (I must
sound reasonable, she thought, oh I must sound reasonable.) "Ever since she got that china ... "

"*You* did it," said Haldar miserably, ignoring her words,
"You make life impossible for me and now you make life
impossible for Maggie."

Maggie's very name inflamed Vera. She cried "Those
were her words! You two have been talking about me!"
She was imprisoned between them.

Haldar gave her a long look and in that look were the
years of frustration, of incomprehension, of joy decayed
and done. He forgot – or did not know – that he had once
cared for her and then had become cruel. He moved
awkwardly and, without speaking, undressed. The sight of
her husband moving awkwardly about the room frightened Vera. His motions seemed to menace her, and indeed
she did not know how near he was to striking her.

"Haldar," she said.
He did not answer.
"Haldar," she cried.
He pulled back the bedclothes.
"Oh Haldar!" she cried again.

He blew out the light, turned on his good side in the bed, away from her, and did not answer.

"Oh Haldar do speak to me!"

But he did not. She saw the awkward hump of his body outlined in the bed against a pale light from the window. He might have been a rock, except that he was compact of misery and anger. She did not dare to touch him and it was well that she did not.

Lying motionless there, he did not know which way to turn within himself. All this damn nonsense, Vera's nagging presence was intolerable to him. At that moment he hated her, but most he hated her presence near him. He began to be swept by a private tornado which, at one touch of his wife's hand, would have torn him apart, raged around the room, and destroyed them both. That was the feeling in the room.

Vera went out, closing the door softly.

The night, and all doors shut, and her rejection, and her self-induced misery grown to devouring proportions took Vera and shook her and led her – where else could she go – toward her destruction and her release. They will see! she cried in her heart, they will see what they have done to me – they will be sorry oh will they be sorry. She would strike at everyone with her death. A dark kind of happiness, a black and stupid rejoicing swept over her and left her. Unworthy unworthy said a phantom among many phantoms. Alan, her little son, was among the phantoms but in her distraction she could not seize and hold him. See those two great planes of wall that crowd down and cut off any escape. I am done! I will go to the lake . . . I must go . . . must go away . . .

The faint light that remained in the western sky did not penetrate the wood. Vera sought the path that lay on the right side of the lake. Trees met overhead, and branches, crossing the unfrequented path, struck at her. All was so dark under the trees that she could not see her way but had to find it with feet that felt and with hands that flinched against the branches. She whimpered as she went because the whimpering seemed to bear her company in the immense hostility of her world.

There is a place down the lake where the rough shores give way to a small beach of muddy sand; trees, less thick there, overhang the edge; the shore shelves rapidly. Vera did not say in her mind "I shall find oblivion there," but dark images crowded her and impelled her to this place to find oblivion. Feeling with her hands, feeling with her feet, whimpering a little, she came to this place and stepped down onto the small muddy sand trip and without pause into the lake.

The first singing stinging clarifying wet cold of the now invisible lake smote Vera but she plunged in and on and the water rose to meet her. In two more steps, in one more plunging step, she would lose control, she would be beyond her depth, struggling then in the wet dark, lost, alone, forever, forever gone. There comes to each of us the moment of return or no return, choose or reject – that moment passes, and no power in heaven or earth can recall it ... she could not, she could not. She turned, splashing, scrambling, falling, rising, sobbing in shame and fear, and made her way to shore and into the black abyss of the woods. She gained the trail which lay where she had left it (could it be possible that she still lived, that this trail, these woods, remained unchanged). Sodden with water she beat her way against the hostile invisible branches, crying "Maggie! Maggie!" as if it were the only word she knew. The sound of this word steadied her, and then she went more quietly.

Forty-Three

THE BAGS were packed, and the yellow bowl was again in the haversack. Maggie lay in the dark despising the turmoil in which she found herself. She must sleep. In the morning she would get the breakfast for everyone as usual. She would tell Haldar, quite shortly, that she was going away. Angus would drive her to Kamloops and she would never come back to Three Loon Lake. Alan, of course, would hardly remember her in years to come.

A knock – was it – and then again. Knock . . . and knock . . . very quiet, very strange, in the dark. Maggie sat up, listening. Something is wrong, she thought, what sort of a knock was that. "Wait," she called to the unknown someone who was standing outside. "I'm coming," she said, and lighted the candle. She pulled on her warm dressing gown and tied the belt quickly. She slipped her feet into her bedroom slippers, took the candle in her hand and went to the door.

She opened the door, holding the candle high, and could not at first see by the flickering flame who or what was there. Vera fixed her eyes on Maggie and moved toward the light. She then stayed still and Maggie, hearing the drip and drip of water dropping on the wooden floor of the veranda and looking on Vera's ghostly face, knew with horror that Vera had tried to drown herself and had not been able.

A room lighted by a candle and in a silent and solitary

place is a world within itself in which there is nothing urban or vulgar. It has a singularity. In this place Maggie and Vera stood, surrounded by the silent dark and lighted by the single candle, and Vera's eyes were fixed with timid melancholy on Maggie's face. Maggie came to herself. Without speaking, and with impassive face, she drew Vera into the cabin and shut the door.

"Oh . . . oh . . . " Vera said with a long shuddering sigh. Maggie, still not speaking, proceeded to strip Vera's wet clothes from her. She took off her own dressing gown and put it upon Vera who continued to shudder. She pushed Vera into a chair, knelt before her and rubbed her legs roughly with a towel. Bending sideways she slipped off her bedroom slippers and put them on Vera's small feet. "I'll make a fire," she said, rising and moving toward the door for wood.

"Don't go! Don't leave me!" cried Vera sharply, but Maggie went outside to the wood box, returned and bent over the stove. Her face had not relented. Her spirit was very sore and sad within her, and still angry, and it seemed to her the least important thing that she should speak and make words, and the most important thing that a fire should burn and warm the cabin and then there would be, somehow, a humanity in the room when the fire was burning, and not just this insoluble misery that had come upon them all from little things, from nothings, really. The fire crackled and burned high in the stove. She stood, barefoot, in her crumpled and unshapely pajamas, looking down at Vera.

Vera seemed to be holding her face together with her two hands, pressing upward over her cheekbones and temples and so tilting her eyes strangely up at the corners.

She said, in fear, with her sad gaze on Maggie "Am I going mad, d'you think?"

"Of course you are not going mad," said Maggie urgently but with her heart failing her, "you'll forget this . . . you'll never do it again . . . you're a happy woman with husband and child and a home. You are not going mad."

"People do," said Vera with dreadful simplicity. Maggie looked away.

"Don't tell Haldar will you . . . don't tell him, he'll think I made you go away. . . . "

"Well, so you did," said Maggie shortly.

Vera fell upon her knees and clasped Maggie round the legs, looking up with her insignificant little face drained of color. "Maggie," she cried, "don't leave me! . . . oh I don't know what's going to happen to me . . . how can I live in this place but he will he will . . . you must stay with me . . . some days I can't bear to see you . . . I hate you I love you I hate you Maggie I love you . . . speak to him for me . . . what shall I do . . . oh help me, you're the only one that can . . . don't ever leave me!"

Maggie, bending, drew Vera up and held her strongly and softly in her arms until the trembling and crying went quiet. She looked in front of her with troubled gaze, through the candlelight into the darkness and into whatever might be beyond the darkness. She could not think what to say to Vera. She did not know what words you use to exorcise the Evil One.

"There then," she said with helpless compassion, patting Vera gently as she held her in her arms, "there then . . . there then . . . "

Forty-Four

VERA LAY in Maggie's bed, the bedclothes pulled high so that only her little face showed. Her thin body lay flat. She looked at the ceiling.

Maggie sat by the stove. She had pulled her coat on over her pajamas. Sometimes it seemed to her that she dozed. She woke with a start and went over to the bed. She laid her hand on Vera's forehead.

"Some cold water Vera?" she said.

Vera sipped obediently and resumed looking at the ceiling. Maggie went back to the stove and put a piece of wood in it. The cabin was wrapped in the dark and quiet of the woods. Maggie dozed and woke again. Vera was speaking.

"Surl," said Vera (it sounded like "Surl"), "always me never Surl," and then she began to talk rapidly.

In the very early morning Maggie dressed and went out. Halfway to Haldar's room she met him. "I can't find Vera," he said in a glowering troubled way, "she didn't come to bed last night. I woke and she wasn't there." He looked hunted, Maggie thought.

"She's with me," she said, choosing her words. "She's ill, Haldar, really ill. She felt ill and needed attention. She came to my cabin."

Haldar's face cleared a little. "What's wrong?" he said uneasily, "what's wrong?"

"She has a temperature, of that I'm sure," said Maggie.

"She's wandering a bit. We'll have to get her down to town, Haldar. Angus must go in and tell the doctor and get the ambulance out. She shouldn't go in a car."

"Ambulance!" exclaimed Haldar, shocked. His anger was falling behind him, and a confusion of remorse, annoyance, anxiety possessed him. The word ambulance seemed to stun him.

"And you'll have to go down with her, Haldar, to the hospital. I'll keep Alan here."

"Me!" said Haldar. "I'm not any good! Couldn't you . . . ? No . . . But how will you manage here single-handed?"

"I've been thinking," said Maggie. They stood in the clearing and the smoke rose from Maggie's chimney. No one else was stirring. "I've been thinking that when you've seen Vera to the hospital, go to the Rogers' and see if young Bill can come out and lend Angus and me a hand. I shall just do the cooking, and the guests will have to look after their own cottages until we get organized. They will. People always help at a time like this. Get the fire going in the kitchen, will you, Haldar." And then as he turned aside, silent, muddled it seemed, she put her hand on his arm. "She may not be as ill as I think. I'll go back."

Haldar said nothing. He felt that it was the time to express gratitude, but he could say nothing. He could have seized her hand and kissed it, but that would be foreign to him and he did not. The confusion of his spirit and some of his anger was still on him. He hobbled to the kitchen and there he did awkwardly what he could. What have we come to, he thought in muddle and anger. Maggie went quickly to the cabin.

Vera had stopped mumbling. She looked at Maggie. "Where were you?" she said. "Don't leave me like that."

"I'll be in and out all day, Vera," said Maggie gently. "You'll soon be better." Vera began to cry.

"A little cup of tea," said Maggie inadequately. "A little cup of tea . . . " (What things we say!)

That was a long hard summer. Toward the end of the

season Maggie received an irascible note from Mrs. Severance.

"Are you coming to Kelowna or are you not coming? Do you expect me to read your mind while you are amusing yourself killing fish or whatever it is you do. Here I am old, venerable and getting madder every day while you keep me waiting. Sleep well, said Enibol."

Maggie smiled as she read (who was Enibol? Some kind of reconciling blessing, she supposed) and wrote briefly and in haste.

"What does she say?" asked Hilda intent on her knitting.

"Poor Maggie! An easy mark. That woman whose name I cannot read has pneumonia. She says, 'I truly have not had time to write. We'll wind up early this year – we're doing very well but are too short-handed, and as soon as I have seen Vera Gunnarsen and know how she is and whether I can leave her, I'll write to you. I'm sure I can come. Be patient dear Nell. Love – Maggie.'"

Mrs. Severance laid the letter down and looked up. "Trouble with Maggie is she's too good to live . . . thank God she has a sense of humor . . . and I shall die with all my imperfections on my head ("And proud of it," said her daughter) . . . proud? not at all, just realistic . . . pride is a base and unattractive sin, I prefer others . . . but I do need to see her . . . she gladdens my eyes, the dear Maggie . . ." Her look rested on Hilda, painstakingly knitting. It was out of character that Hilda should knit, and it piqued and amused Mrs. Severance that she should knit. She did not so often think of the Swamp Angel now but there were times, such as this, when her hand reached out and then stopped, defrauded.

"I suppose it's a sign of character that you are beginning to knit at your age (pass me the cigarettes). I commend you, Hilda, but you do fidget me, poking and poking like that. I wish now that pregnancy had affected me in that way and then I would poke too, but it didn't." She had to vent her small impatience about the uncertain holiday on something, and Hilda's knitting would do; yet she did not annoy her daughter any more. Hilda only smiled and said, "I'm good, and you're jealous," and went on knitting slowly and with absorption. Habit persists, but the two women were more deeply equable than they used to be.

Forty-Five

Hilda was suffering from morning sickness.

"Rufus," she said, "you'll have to take Mother to the train," and sped to the bathroom.

Albert's beard had turned out to be reddish and this had invested Albert with something of the ruthless-bandit-lover. Albert, unaware of this, moved in a duality of Albert-Rufus, becoming, later, entirely Rufus.

An hour later Albert telephoned to his wife.

"How are you feeling?" said Rufus.

"Better," said Hilda faintly. "Was she all right?"

"She was in high spirits . . . "

"Had she a hat?"

"I didn't notice . . . no, I don't think so."

Hilda made a sound.

"What?" said Rufus.

"Nothing," said Hilda, "don't forget the chops darling." At the word chops she lay down again. She would feel better later in the day. People said Really Hilda you look lovely. How enchanting, how devastating the future of humanity. She felt she had always known this, which was not the case.

Forty-Six

I SUPPOSE," said Mrs. Severance speaking with sardonic benevolence, "that you thought that once out of that house on Capitol Hill, once away from Edward Vardoe, once out into the fresh air, everything would be easy. My dear sap, it never is. Don't you know that, Maggie?"

"I do know it."

"Escape to a desert island if you like, but I tell you that the island mentality is a trouble factory. And look at St. Anthony what happened to him."

"I'm not escaping ... now."

"I don't care for fresh air myself except for the purpose of breathing. I exist here ... and here ... " Mrs. Severance touched her heart and her head. "Everything of any importance happens indoors ... "

"Oh it does not!" said Maggie.

" ... including eating and sleeping. Life is the damndest thing what it can think up for people," continued Mrs. Severance, "but I wouldn't have missed it ... the places you do contrive to get yourself into, Maggie ... are you going to stay there and spend your life drying off fools who get wet on purpose? Really."

"It won't happen again," said Maggie mildly, "and no one knows about Vera – except you. They just think she had pneumonia, and of course she did. She's better."

"You know nothing about it. You don't know *what* will happen," said Mrs. Severance behind a cloud of smoke.

"Look at Philip's family. They all started life as infants and that guaranteed them nothing. Take the eldest brother Monty. He was a gentle anarchist. When he was staying with us, the evil of the world had become too much for him and he started one night to throw himself off a cliff. What a night! Then he found that he had forgotten his false teeth so he came back to the house to get them. When he got his teeth in he reconsidered. Later he became very respectable and dropped us. He married a millionaire biscuit manufacturer's daughter and died a year or two ago of old age and in affluence, surrounded by a gaggle of grandchildren who never would have existed if it hadn't been for Monty's false teeth. Percy went to jail. Margaret was an angel and her life was one long committee meeting on prison reform. Henry was a stuffed shirt. My Philip had a passion for the circus and for archaeology and no sense of public responsibility at all. He ran away to a circus and that, of course, was when he saw me. . . . Do you know what love is, Maggie? Somehow I think you do."

Maggie did not interrupt Mrs. Severance who was thinking out loud and telling her the things that Maggie had not known and that she had long wanted to know. Mrs. Severance reached across the table for a package, opened it and, squinting a little, lighted a cigarette from her stub. She looked up into the smoke.

"Philip had ideas about marriage. He had a lot of ideas and I learned about ideas. He was a singularly monogamous man but did not approve of what he thought were the 'bonds' of matrimony so we did not marry. I have never regretted anything in my life with Philip, not even that – I don't suppose Hilda knows it. At the time I should like to have been married because I believe in marriage and for my father and mother's sake who were respectable people though they did not go to church except in theory. It's difficult in the circus. It hurt them a lot and it really upset Philip's parents. Frankly I found it hard. I think they never got over the feeling that I had seduced Philip and I don't wonder – 'a girl from the circus!' Well, look at all those children – issuing from the same womb, all different and all dead, and you sit there and tell me that something will or will not happen again! Everything happens again and it's never the same. Let us go out. You should take the air."

They walked slowly together, Mrs. Severance leaning her great weight on her stick. Yes, she has aged, thought Maggie.

"I sit on top of my little mound of years," said Mrs. Severance, "and it is natural and reasonable that I should look back, and I look back and round and I see the miraculous interweaving of creation . . . the everlasting web . . . and I see a stone and a word and this stub," and she threw down the stub of her cigarette, "and the man who made it, joined to the bounds of creation, and I see God everywhere. And Edward Vardoe (Albert says he seems to be married or something – did you know?) and your little Chinese boy and the other little boy and you and me and who knows what. We are all in it together. 'No Man is an Island, I am involved in Mankinde,' and we have no immunity and we may as well realize it. You won't be immune ever at that lake Maggie" (nor anywhere else, thought Maggie. No one is). "I have just a few convictions left and I hope to die before I lose them. But when Albert says What do you believe and I say I believe in faith and Albert says Faith in what, I can't tell him. Because when you try to put faith into words, the words are hollow. Faith in God is my support, and it makes old age bearable and happy, and fearless I think. But that is not why I believe. It's funny, Maggie," (the old woman, walking slowly, was very happy in her communications to Maggie who listened with affection) "but Albert comes to see *his* mother-in-law and Hilda goes to see *her* mother-in-law for choice. Being pregnant suits Hilda. She looks happy. She will bring up her children by rule. She has bought a book on psychology – she's too damn serious – but Albert will leaven the lump of parenthood for their children . . . perhaps if I'd had some books on psychology Hilda would have been happier. But, with me, it was Philip or Hilda, Philip or Hilda, I knew I was in the web, I did the best I could in the web, and it takes God himself to be fair to two different people at once."

Maggie almost jumped at these words which had risen so often in her own mind.

"Let's go in now," said Mrs. Severance. "It's nice being together, isn't it. Three more days. You're good to me Maggie."

"Nell . . . ! Does Alberto really look after you? He's not too much of a care?"

"Alberto? No no. I like him and his absurdness. He comes and goes regardless and that suits me. He does what he can. He comes and bursts into song. I must say I usually dislike the human voice raised in song, especially in opera, but Alberto with his hand on his heart, pouring it out to the ceiling, pleases me. With him it seems the natural function of a voice. Like birds . . . yes?" she said, turning.

A young woman was at the door "Would one of you ladies be Mrs. Lloyd?" she asked.

"I would," said Maggie.

"Wanted on long distance," said the young woman and vanished.

Maggie went, and returned.

"Nell," she said, "I have to go back. At once. That was Henry Corder. In a state. It's Vera."

A look that was a smile, comprehending, skeptical, came over Mrs. Severance's face. She raised her hands, her shoulders.

"You see!" she said.

"Will you be all right, how'll you manage?" said Maggie, pausing. (What was it Vera. What happened – what did you do?)

"Me? My good woman! How'll I manage? I managed in Troy."

"Troy? What has Troy to do with it," said Maggie

gently, looking at her old friend. She did not wish to say to her But now, you're old.

"What has this Vera done now?" asked Mrs. Severance.

"I don't know. Perhaps it's a relapse, perhaps not. Henry's only got one cover-all word for everything from a headache to a hemorrhage, she's 'sick.' And he hates long-distance telephoning."

"Why, *Why* . . . Maggie," said Mrs. Severance vehemently, looking intently at Maggie's face, "do you stay with these people? You're absurd. You'll always carry their load. Go to that Cunningham place!"

"Alan's my joy and will be," said Maggie equably, "and you'd like Henry Corder."

"I don't like any one of the whole lot of them. Oh go and pack your things," said the old woman testily. She pulled a package of cigarettes from her pocket, drew out a cigarette slowly, and lighted it. She was annoyed with Vera. Illness was inopportune. Soon the fresh prevailing wind in her mind arose and blew away irrelevancies. Sitting still, inhaling too deeply and looking through the smoke, hearing Maggie in the next room getting ready to leave her, she thought The unhappy Vera; housebound without an opening window; hellbound, I think. Poor Vera. Poor people.

Forty-Seven

S OON AS spring's here we'll take her up to the lake."
"Wait till she says she wants to go, Haldar," said
Maggie.

"That's the finest air in the world for what ailed her! I
asked Doc Haines and he said. Two thousand feet above
Kamloops, good and dry! We'll take her right up and fix
the dee lux cabin for her."

But Maggie only said again, "Wait till she says she wants
to go, Haldar."

"She seems kinda quiet don't you think Maggie?"

"Give her time."

(And could Vera bear to view that scene again? And
could she bear that Maggie knows what she knows? What
can Vera do? Oh want can I do? Something has changed in
me and I am lost.)

"I think," said Maggie at last, "f'rinstance, Alan and I
can do a little more petting, a little helping. And Henry –
you and Haldar too . . . "

"Gosh . . . me? . . . " exclaimed Henry Corder in
alarm. "I couldn't pet anybody – never done such a thing
in all my life!"

"I'll teach you Henry," laughed Maggie. Haldar did not
laugh. In his mind was the dark lamentable knowledge
that some years ago something had slipped, just a little, at
first. Perhaps it was Vera's fault. Perhaps it was his own
fault. Perhaps it was that damn hip. By this time he stood

alone and he did not know where Vera stood; if she were another woman, and not his wife, he would not care where she stood.

He left Henry and Maggie talking beside the gate and limped back to the house. Alan came running home in the dusk.

"Come son," said Haldar. "Let's go in and see how your mother's getting along."

"Sure," said Alan, breathless.

Henry Corder turned and looked back at them.

"Can you work it somehow Maggie so's them two gits together?" he said.

"*I* can't Henry. Maybe Alan can without ever knowing it. Perhaps there's a way. I think there might be a way. It isn't easy and it's not going to be easy."

"I'll tell the cockeyed world," said Henry Corder. He meditated, spitting – from time to time – into the night.

Then "It's cold," he said, and they went in.

One day there came a letter.

Dear Maggie

I am very very sorry to tell you that Mother died on Friday. I suppose it could be called an easy going. The week before she had what must have been a small stroke. Alberto was there. Then she had a bad one. Mrs. Spink telephoned the doctor and she tried to get me, poor Mrs. Spink you can imagine and I was out with Baby so she got Rufus and Rufus went up at once and he is sure that she knew him. Rufus and Mother were very very fond of each other and I'm so thankful he was with her. When I got there she knew nothing and next day she was gone. I feel Maggie that I ought to say some of the sad conventional things about Mother it seems only right but I can't because Mother's life was complete and to say anything else would be phony and that's one thing she couldn't bear. She loved you Maggie and I think you know she wanted you to do something or other about the Swamp Angel. It feels strange. The funeral was yesterday. Very small.

Baby is such a darling and so good. You should see him. We call him Monty after Montgomery, Rufus's mother's maiden name. I will send you a photograph. Now that we have changed his formula . . .

Can this be Hilda Severance, the scornful one, daughter of Nell Severance? No, this is Hilda Cousins, blender of bottles, mother of Monty, who is writing.

So Nell has gone now. She is my greatest friend and the friend of my spirit. Henry and Haldar and Vera and Alan – they're my people but not of the spirit like Nell. What a life she had lived, thought Maggie, standing with the letter in her hand. Even if she had never moved from her house, what a life she had lived, the worldly unworldly woman. For me there is no one like her. Maggie did not mourn for Mrs. Severance. There is mourning and missing.

As Maggie and Angus drove up the hill past the Iron Mask mine the country became more delicately, coolly vernal. Strong fresh green had spread in the valley of the Thompson River. A pale frigid green had now begun to flow over the dun-colored upper levels. There still were distant pockets of snow. Here, once more, they drove past the great solitary bull pines with their strongly hatched and corrugated bark – all the delights of this country spoke afresh to Maggie – swelling hills, wild and widespread sage, look! there is a coyote and his coat is the same dun color as the hill on which he runs purposefully about his business. He vanishes. This was Maggie's third year in. Breathe this sagey air! See, a bluebird! Floating cloud, drifting scent, tree, wild creature, curving fleeting hill – each made its own statement to Maggie in the imperishable spring.

The back part of the car was piled with supplies, tools, nails, two sacks of cement, new stove piping. Angus cleared his throat and said "Saw Mr. Carruthers at the post office yesterday. Him or the other Mr. Carruthers going out to the ranch Friday. Said he'd call around n see n if I hadn't picked up Mr. Gunnarsen he'd bring him out. I said Okay. But I guess I'd better get back Wednesday or Thursday n then we'll know what else we need n tell Mr. Gunnarsen n give him a chance to order. Mr. Carruthers said he'd come around next week n get me started on the new cabins."

"Good," said Maggie, and then she said warmly, "Bless you Angus, you're a wholly satisfactory boy!"

Angus drove neatly along the winding trail. He was greatly astonished to hear Mrs. Lloyd call him a holy boy. Gosh, he thought, but he did not like to argue. Then he said "Thank you Mrs. Lloyd." Looking ahead through his thick spectacles he felt that he would indeed try to be holy although he did not quite know what Mrs. Lloyd meant. However he trusted her because she was Mrs. Lloyd and that was enough.

"When we get there," said Maggie who would have been surprised by all this, " – oh stop a minute, here's the signpost we made, it's stood the winter well! – when we get there we'll open up everything right away and start the fires everywhere. I'll do the kitchen one – but get a boat out for me first and a couple of oars – I want to go on the lake for about half an hour before we settle to work, and by the time I'm back the stove'll be going well and I'll give us lunch."

"Okay Mrs. Lloyd."

"That little cubbyhole Alan's always slept in, it's too small for him now and anyway we need it for stores. You two boys will have to go in together in that first cabin – the little old one – when they come up and till we get things going. You put your things in that cabin Angus, and when I've aired the blankets you make up your bed. But be sure you make your own fire first of all and have your cabin good and warm by bedtime won't you?"

"Okay."

"And if you've any ideas about things as you go around just make a note of them in that little notebook of yours and tell me will you."

"Sure."

Things were falling into place; thus and so they should be. This was Maggie's own sphere. This she could do well, with Angus. As for Angus, he was no longer the middle child, the brother surrounded and eclipsed by the family. He was a man of eighteen who had worked at the lake all summer and had operated a taxi all winter and who knew more how to go about things, and did not always have to ask now; and he kept a notebook. Three times during the winter he had driven up with another boy with a cute little power saw in the back seat and had cut wood; and there was all that lumber laying there for the new cabins, brought in from a sawmill in the hills but, he thought, he daresnt touch it till Mr. Carruthers showed him how. At the lake last summer very important old guys who came to fish, like Mr. Roberts and Mr. Cunningham, seemed to think he knew about things. He was regarded as a real person and responsible there by those solid guys and by Mrs. Lloyd and the Gunnarsen family. He was more of a person than he would be on Pender Street. Wait a couple of years and get Dad up here to see; bet he'll be surprised. Angus is right. A man, and even a man's dog, has special quality and value in a landscape with trees.

After Maggie had lighted the fire she went down to the lake with the Angel in her pocket. She loosed the boat and rowed out into the lake. She rowed easily and with pleasure. The pull on the oars felt good throughout her body. At last she looked around her and shipped her oars. She picked up the revolver from where she had laid it in the bottom of the boat.

Maggie sits in the rowboat turning the Angel in her

hands and she knows that this little gun has a virtue which was more than pearl and nickel to old Mrs. Severance; it has its own properties and its small immortality. That is why Maggie handles the Swamp Angel and looks at it curiously and thoughtfully as she sits there gently moving with the slight movement of the boat on the water in the fine fresh air; and that is why she thinks that this is a rite of some kind which she is about to perform. Just the same, this revolver is far too good to be thrown away.

The Swamp Angel in its eighty years or so had caused death and astonishment and jealousy and affection and one night it frightened Edward Vardoe on Maggie's behalf, although Maggie does not know that, and soon it will be gone. It will be a memory, and then not even a memory, for there will be no one to remember it. Yet does the essence of all custom and virtue perish? How can she know. Quick . . . waste no time . . . you must go back to work . . . Angus is hungry . . . throw that little gun into the lake at once.

Maggie did not drop the Swamp Angel over the side of the boat into the water. She stood in the boat and with her strong arm she threw the Angel up into the air, higher than even Nell Bigley of the Juggling Bigleys had ever tossed it. It made a shining parabola in the air, turning downward – turning, turning, catching the sunlight, hitting the surface of the lake, sparkling down into the clear water, vanishing amidst breaking bubbles in the water, sinking down among the affrighted fish, settling in the ooze. When all was still the fish, who had fled, returned, flickering, weaving curiously over the Swamp Angel. Then flickering, weaving, they resumed their way.

Maggie, turning, rowing quickly back to the lodge, had the bow of the boat pointed toward the lodge and the stern pointed toward the farther and ever receding shore of the lake, the hills. The far shore (like Mrs. Severance) would recede until it was nearly out of sight, but it would still be there. There were certain things that Maggie could not settle. Would a recovered but enfeebled Vera return to the

lake and to the poignant sight of that memorable and
melancholy shore? And if she did not return, could Haldar so far bend his own strong will as to stay with her in
town? Maggie thought (but she was not thinking of these
things now) that they would both return – yet she did not
know. She had, during the winter, arrived at a conclusion
that, for better for worse, there were certain things that
two people must resolve – however mistakenly, however
uncertainly – between themselves. Outside influence
would not avail. The springs of action, deeply hidden,
were too difficult for her. And so Maggie had applied
herself to the matters in hand. Now she stopped rowing
for a moment to get her direction, and looked back
toward the lodge. She saw the stocky comfortable figure of
Angus moving from cabin to cabin. Smoke had begun to
rise from the stovepipes of the cabins, and smoke flowed
up abundantly into the still air from the kitchen chimney.
Maggie turned again, took the oars, and rowed hard,
straight in the direction of the lodge.

Afterword

BY GEORGE BOWERING

Ethel Wilson lived in a posh neighbourhood of Vancouver. She was the wife of a prominent doctor, and employed immigrant servants. Her first book was published in her sixtieth year, her last book fourteen years later, though Wilson would live to be almost ninety-three. Her few public remarks about writing appear quite unassuming. In her 1959 essay, "A Cat Among the Falcons," she referred to literary critics as high-flying falcons and herself as a "country cat" sitting and looking out a window.

Her early critics took her at her word. They did not know, perhaps, that she was an expert fly fisherwoman as is her protagonist Maggie Lloyd. Even her supporters, most of them men who matured in the school of modern realism, tended to patronize her, presenting her as an unambitious chronicler, innocent of intellectual and moral matters but somehow gifted in limning character.

Most of these commentators regretted certain faults in Wilson's writing style. These included inconsistency, irritating changes of pace, and above all "authorial intrusion." None explained how an author can be said to intrude upon her own invention. They saw her direct remarks to her reader as slips into Victorianism. They should have re-read her feline essay, noticing that the fiction writers she cites are the innovators, what hurried critics call the "stylists." They might have noticed that she praises the "incandescence in a lighted mind" to be found in Sheila Watson's newly published *The Double Hook*.

A remarkable exception among the early critics was Helen Sonthoff ("The Novels of Ethel Wilson, "*Canadian Literature*, 1965), who found treasure just where the fellows were finding lapses. Hers is one of our great essays. It locates Ethel Wilson among those writers who make their readers experience the writing, and Sonthoff quotes Gertrude Stein, who said that the sentence should "make you know yourself knowing it." Ethel Wilson, whenever she was asked to say what it was that the young writer had to learn, suggested the sentence.

Once in a while you will find a Wilson sentence that strikes you as odd. It might have a crack in it; it might have forgotten which way it was going. When you find a little oddity in a Wilson sentence, you should question the seeming simplicity that has gone before. You could be afforded a glimpse of the moral, philosophical world of which Wilson was supposed to be unmindful. In the midst of the world the author has made familiar, you might suffer some defamiliarizing. At that moment you may get irritated and fault the narrative's professionalism – or you may sense the presence of a cat, and feel the hairs on the back of your neck rise.

Wilson's purpose is not cheery. When you are least expecting it, she lets you see a moment of something dark, something Joseph Conrad's river-travelling Marlow might have seen between the wide leaves. Consider the idyllic scene of Maggie's fishing the bright Similkameen River:

> Maggie continued to cast. In the pleasure of casting over this lively stream she forgot – as always when she was fishing – her own existence. Suddenly came a strike, and the line ran out, there was a quick radiance and splashing above the water downstream. At the moment of the strike, Maggie became a co-ordinating creature of wrists and fingers and reel and rod and line and tension and the small trout, leaping, darting, leaping. She landed the fish, took out the

hook, slipped in her thumb, broke back the small neck, and the leaping rainbow thing was dead. A thought as thin and cruel as a pipefish cut through her mind. The pipefish slid through and away. It would return.

In less than a page the cruel thought does return, and it brings Edward Vardoe with it. For the second time in the novel we are brushed with the thought of "humiliation" that drove Maggie to leave him, the guilt in deciding to cease her "outraged endurance of the nights' hateful assaults and the days' wakings in a passing of time where daily and nightly repetition marked no passing of time." As in our reading of Conrad, we do not know with certainty, yet we think we've seen the edge of a universal darkness. When Nell Severance suggests to Edward Vardoe that in his own darkest vengeful mind "murder would be a pleasure," he does not contradict her. Neither he nor his estranged wife is an innocent traveller; nor is their creator. More and more as Wilson composed her fictions, her characters were compelled to consider unexplainable death and the fear that wreathes it like vapour around the fragments of a train wreck.

Wilson's travelling protagonists leave the seeming unity and comfort of family to discover disappointing and frightening chaos, and set about creating an uncloistered order. Remember the Ancient Mariner, that returned traveller: with thoughtless murderous skill he brings down the albatross; when he blesses the watersnakes *unaware*, the stinking bird falls from his neck and the narrative wind arises. You will remember that Maggie *forgets* her own existence just before she despatches the little trout and feels the darkness "cut through her mind." Now recall that verb in this "authorial intrusion":

> There is a beautiful action. It has an operative grace. It is when one, seeing some uneasy sleeper cold and without a cover, goes away, finds and fetches a blanket, bends down, and covers the sleeper because the sleeper is a living being and is cold. He then returns to his work, forgetting that he

has performed this small act of compassion. He will receive
neither praise nor thanks. It does not matter who the sleeper
may be. That is a beautiful action which is divine and
human in posture and intention and self-forgetfulness.
Maggie was compassionate and perhaps she would be able to
serve Vera Gunnarsen in this way, forgetting that she did so,
and expecting neither praise nor thanks – or perhaps she
would not.

The last five words epitomize Ethel Wilson's noted
"tone," and serve to attract the reader who wants to feel,
paradoxically, closer to the seemingly detached writer.
Wilson knew that she was producing that paradox, and
she employed it as well in the telling she had to do about
her subjects: "all fly-fishermen are bound closely together
by the strong desire to be apart, solitary upon the lake, the
stream."

Paradox, or at least contradiction, for certain metaphor,
is signalled in the novel's title. Observing that range from
primordial slime to divine flight, one might expect a story
of triumphant emergence, but I do not think that the
angel emerges. I think that no matter how compas-
sionately Maggie acts, even in the Christian terms that the
book clearly suggests, the pipefish still swims in her mind.
A swamp angel is not necessarily a gun. The dictionary
that Wilson alerts us to on her first page tells us that the
swamp angel can be an eremite in the bog, or another
name for the hermit thrush, that feathery song.

Birds are important to Wilson's fictions. They fly in
formations, break their necks against windows, carry messages quicker than the symbols Mrs. Severance complains
of. Fifty brown birds fly in this book's first sentence, and
Mrs. Vardoe (or the narrator) asks what they are. Perhaps
they are swamp angels; certainly they are "birds returning
in migration," probably ironic precursors of this still
earth-held Vardoe woman. They are recalled in the fish
that return to the water above the ooze into which the gun
settles in the penultimate paragraph. "Things are falling
into place," one reads a page earlier.

Maggie Lloyd's place is somewhere between the birds and the fish. She will never fly further than her flight from Vardoe, and she will never live all the time among the seals and porpoises or in Three Loon Lake, no matter what her avatars say. The fish do not reside in a swamp and the birds are not angels. Take that delimiting a step further: birds such as eagles eat fish and take them flying; people such as Maggie Lloyd make flies out of feathers and feed trout to their death.

Look at those birds and fish again. For Maggie the birds are seen and the fish are imagined. For Ethel Wilson they are all imagined, and so what are they for the reader?

Ethel Wilson the writer wanted two things that are opposite and necessary to one another. She genuinely loved the physicality of British Columbia, and used her great sentences to make it brightly visible. If the rivers and lakes are to become allegorical landscape, that will be permitted, but they will live before the imagining eye first. There is also a dark universe, however, that turns and looms outside the range of the human eye. As dogs and other animals sense oncoming earthquakes, Wilson's protagonist and reader, easing into the pre-visual world of nature, enter the dream of Eddie Vardoe, whose face becomes the face of a child and then a sharp-toothed mink screaming in the forest.

"Going fishing?" everyone asks Maggie. "Yes, I am," she replies pleasantly. Like any novelist, a fisherwoman can tie a practised fly, search the best rainbow shoal, and still be in the dark as to what she may, with her single hook, hook.

But in fishing she offers a faith in order, in a not-quite-predictable order. About her earlier books, especially *Hetty Dorval*, Wilson was sometimes upbraided for her use of coincidences, especially coincidental meetings, in her plots. In *Swamp Angel*, an often recurvate text, she responds to that criticism through the words of the never-shy Mrs. Severance, who tells Albert Cousins that she believes in two things: coincidence and faith. That sounds a little like the paradoxical reality that Maggie the questor comes to learn. Is a coincidence an island of random order in a sea of chaos, or is coincidence chaotic itself? To the realist non-Jungian critic it is a cheat or a failure of vision. To a person to any degree religious it can look like evidence of supernal regard for the mortal world.

In any case critics have always held *Swamp Angel* to be superior to its predecessors in terms of authorial control. This is so partly because, despite her probable opinion on the matter, Wilson cut back on coincidence. This novel's plot is articulated by illnesses, accidents and injuries. Plot is developed and characters are constructed by these reminders of human frailty and fallibility. They start with the battlefield death of Tom Lloyd, and include, among others, the fall of Nell Severance in the street, Haldar Gunnarsen's car wreck, and the sudden storm that brings an end to Mr. Cunningham's strength. Each event has a part in bringing Maggie to her place in the boat on the lake, on the way to the lodge where the smoke is rising from the chimneys. Of the accidents and the tangles of emotion that have got her there, Maggie has told herself simply, "life is like that – if it's not one thing it's another." Wilson gave her that common language to keep her normal, to show us that all her compassion and personal strength are simply human possibility, not the attributes of a literary hero. The epigraph for *Mrs. Golightly* quotes Edwin Muir on the world we have to inhabit: "a difficult country, and our home."

Most of Wilson's stories are about the problem of home, and most of these are about a girl or woman looking for the meaning of the term. For Maggie, the house in which she had lived with Eddie Vardoe was "home" as only a geographical designation. It had been a fake haven for the younger woman who had become widow, orphan and childless all at once. So, like a fish, she goes upstream to something she seems in the darkness to recognize. In the short Chapter 5, Maggie Vardoe is reborn as Maggie Lloyd, and in her snug cabin finds her first comfort as this new child. The word "home" comes from a root meaning to lie down. In Vardoe's bed she lay in anguish every night. Here

The cabin was a safe small world enclosing her. She put out
a hand, groped on the stand beside her bed, took up the
small yellow bowl, ran her thumb round its smooth glaze
like a drowsy child feeling its toy. How lovely the sound of
the wind in the fir trees. She fell asleep.

The next day she rides through the town of Hope.

But the lodge on Three Loon Lake is surrounded by
dark forest, and as the people who live there know,
unpleasant things can happen any time. The reader
should be on guard as well. If you were ever in a mind to
swallow the fish story about the author's self-image, the
country cat far from the nearest pigeons, look again at the
end to the scene of the fawn and the kitten:

> The kitten awoke, completely aware of birds in the woods.
> She jumped down and trotted along the veranda and onto
> the ground. Then, flattening herself, extending herself paw by
> predatory paw, she passed crouching into the forest.

Swamp Angel is a short novel and a highly complex
one. On re-reading it we are rewarded with the assurance
that we will never be able to tell anyone what it is all
about. Wilson's feigned simplicity is the most complicated
trick of all. For a careful reader the text is as difficult as
this world our home.

BY ETHEL WILSON

FICTION
Hetty Dorval (1947)
The Innocent Traveller (1949)
The Equations of Love (1952)
Swamp Angel (1954)
Love and Salt Water (1956)
Mrs. Golightly and Other Stories (1961)

SELECTED WRITINGS
Ethel Wilson: Stories, Essays, and Letters
[ed. David Stouck] (1987)

New Canadian Library
The Best of Canadian Writing

Also Available in the New Canadian Library

Margaret Atwood
The Edible Woman
Afterword by Linda Hutcheon

Surfacing
Afterword by
Marie-Claire Blais

Yves Beauchemin
The Alley Cat
Afterword by Kenneth Radu

Earle Birney
Turvey
Afterword by Al Purdy

Marie-Claire Blais
Mad Shadows
Afterword by Daphne Marlatt

*A Season in the Life
of Emmanuel*
Afterword by Nicole Brossard

Fred Bodsworth
Last of the Curlews
Afterword by Graeme Gibson

Frances Brooke
*The History of
Emily Montague*
Afterword by
Lorraine McMullen

Ernest Buckler
*The Mountain and
the Valley*
Afterword by Robert Gibbs

Morley Callaghan
More Joy in Heaven
Afterword by Margaret Avison

Such Is My Beloved
Afterword by Milton Wilson

*They Shall Inherit
the Earth*
Afterword by Ray Ellenwood

Canadian Poetry
*From the Beginnings
Through the First
World War*
Afterword by Carole Gerson
and Gwendolyn Davies

NCL – A Series Worth Collecting

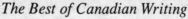 **New Canadian Library**
The Best of Canadian Writing

Also Available in the New Canadian Library

Leonard Cohen

Beautiful Losers
Afterword by Stan Dragland

The Favourite Game
Afterword by Paul Quarrington

Ralph Connor

Glengarry School Days
Afterword by John Lennox

The Man from Glengarry
Afterword by Alison Gordon

Sara Jeannette Duncan

The Imperialist
Afterword by
Janette Turner Hospital

Marian Engel

Bear
Afterword by Aritha van Herk

Sylvia Fraser

Pandora
Afterword by Lola Lemire
Tostevin

Mavis Gallant

*The Moslem Wife and
Other Stories*
Afterword by Mordecai Richler

Frederick Philip Grove

Fruits of the Earth
Afterword by Rudy Wiebe

Over Prairie Trails
Afterword by Patrick Lane

A Search for America
Afterword by W.H. New

Settlers of the Marsh
Afterword by
Kristjana Gunnars

T.C. Haliburton

The Clockmaker
Afterword by
Robert L. McDougall

Paul Hiebert

Sarah Binks
Afterword by Charles Gordon

Jack Hodgins

*The Invention of the
World*
Afterword by
George McWhirter

Spit Delaney's Island
Afterword by
Robert Bringhurst

NCL – A Series Worth Collecting

New Canadian Library
The Best of Canadian Writing

Also Available in the New Canadian Library

NCL – A Series Worth Collecting

New Canadian Library
The Best of Canadian Writing

M&S

Also Available in the New Canadian Library

NCL – A Series Worth Collecting

New Canadian Library
The Best of Canadian Writing

M&S

Also Available in the New Canadian Library

NCL – A Series Worth Collecting

New Canadian Library
The Best of Canadian Writing

Also Available in the New Canadian Library

The Tin Flute
Afterword by Philip Stratford

*Where Nests the
Water Hen*
Afterword by Sandra Birdsell

Windflower
Afterword by Phyllis Webb

Ernest Thompson Seton
*Wild Animals I Have
Known*
Afterword by David Arnason

Robert Stead
Grain
Afterword by Laurie Ricou

Catherine Parr Traill
*The Backwoods of
Canada*
Afterword by D.M.R. Bentley

Sheila Watson
The Double Hook
Afterword by F.T. Flahiff

Rudy Wiebe
*The Blue Mountains
of China*
Afterword by Eva-Marie Kröller

*The Temptations of
Big Bear*
Afterword by Robert Kroetsch

Ethel Wilson
The Equations of Love
Afterword by Alice Munro

Hetty Dorval
Afterword by Northrop Frye

The Innocent Traveller
Afterword by P.K. Page

Love and Salt Water
Afterword by Anne Marriott

*Mrs. Golightly and Other
Stories*
Afterword by David Stouck

Swamp Angel
Afterword by George Bowering

Adele Wiseman
Crackpot
Afterword by
Margaret Laurence

NCL – A Series Worth Collecting